The
Lady and Sada San

Beautiful even in her pallor

The
Lady and Sada San

A Sequel to
The Lady of the Decoration

By

Frances Little

New York
The Century Co.
1912

TO
ELLEN CHURCHILL SEMPLE
AND
CHARLOTTE SMITH

MY FELLOW WANDERERS THROUGH THE ORIENT

The Lady and Sada San

The Lady and Sada San

On the High Seas. June, 1911.

Mate:

You once told me, before you went to Italy, that after having been my intimate relative all these years, you had drawn a red line through the word surprise. Restore the abused thing to its own at once. You will need it when the end of this letter is reached. I have left Kentucky after nine years of stay-at-home happiness, and once again I am on my way to Japan—this time in wifely disobedience to Jack's wishes.

What do you think that same Jack has "gone and done"! Of course he

is right. That is the provoking part
of Jack; it always turns out that he is
in the right. Two months ago he went
to some place in China which, from its
ungodly name, should be in the fur-
thermost parts of a wilderness. Per-
haps you have snatched enough time
from guarding the kiddies from a pre-
mature end in Como to read a head-
line or so in the home papers. If by
some wonderful chance, between baby
prattle, bumps and measles, they have
given you a moment's respite, then you
know that the Government has grown
decidedly restless for fear the energetic
and enterprising bubonic or pneumonic
germ might take passage on some of
the ships from the Orient. So it is
fortifying against invasion. The Government, knowing Jack's indomitable
determination to learn everything
knowable about the private life and

4

character of a given germ, asked him to join several other men it is sending out to get information, provided of course the germ does n't get them first.

Jack read me the official-looking document one night between puffs of his after-dinner pipe.

Another surprise awaits you. For once in my life I had nothing to say. Possibly it is just as well for the good of the cause that the honorable writer of the letter could not see how my thoughts looked.

I glanced about our little den, aglow with soft lights; everything in it seemed to smile. Well, as you know it, Mate, I do not believe even you realize the blissfulness of the hours of quiet comradeship we have spent there. With the great know-it-all old world shut out, for joyful years we have dwelt together in a home-made paradise. And yet it seemed just then as if I were dwelling in a home-made Other Place.

The difference in the speed of time depends on whether love is your guest or not.

The thought of the briefest interruption to my content made me feel like cold storage. A break in happiness is sometimes hard to mend. The blossom does not return to the tree after the storm, no matter how beautiful the sunshine; and the awful fear of the faintest echo of past sorrow made my heart as numb as a snowball. To the old terror of loneliness was added fear for Jack's safety. But I did not do what you naturally would prophesy. After seeing the look on Jack's face I changed my mind, and my protest was the silent kind that says so much. It was lost! Already Jack had gone into one of his trances, as he does whenever there is a possibility of bearding a brand-new microbe in its den, whether it is in his own country or one beyond the seas. In body he was in a padded chair with all the comforts of home and a charming wife within speaking distance. In spirit he was in dust-laden China, joyfully following the trail of the wandering germ. Later on, when Jack came to, we talked it over. I truly remembered your warnings on the danger of impetuosity; for I choked off every hasty word and gave my consent for Jack to go. Then I cried half the night because I had.

We both know that long ago Jack headed for the topmost rung of a very tall scientific ladder. Sometimes my enthusiasm as chief booster and encourager has failed, as when it meant absence and risk. Though I have known women who specialized in renunciation, till they were the only happy people in the neighborhood, its charms have never lured me into any violent sacrifice. Here was my chance and I firmly refused to be the millstone to ornament Jack's neck.

You might know, Mate? I was hoping all the time that he would find it quite impossible to leave such a nice biddable wife at home. But I learn something new about Jack every day. After rather heated discussion it was decided that I should stay in the little home. That is, the heat and the discussion was all on my side. The decision lay in the set of Jack's mouth, despite the tenderness in his eyes. He thought the risks of the journey too great for me; the hardships of the rough life too much. Dear me! Will men never learn that hardship and risk are double cousins to loneliness, and not even related to love by marriage?

But just as well paint on water as to argue with a scientist when he has reached a conclusion.

Besides, said Jack, the fatherly Government has no intention that petticoats, even hobbled ones, should be flitting around while the habits and the methods of the busy insect were being examined through a microscope or a telescope. The choice of instrument depending, of course, upon the activity of the bug.

Black Charity was to be my chief-of-police and comforter-in-general. Parties—house, card and otherwise—were to be my diversion, and I was to make any little trips I cared for. Well, that's just what I am doing. Off course, there might be a difference of opinion as to whether a journey from Kentucky to Japan is a *little* trip.

I am held by a vague uneasiness to-day. Possibly it's because I am not certain as to Jack's attitude, when he learns through my letter, which is sailing along with me, that I am going to Japan to be as near him as possible. I hope he will appreciate my thoughtfulness in saving him all the bother of saying no. Or it might be that my slightly dampened spirits come from the discussion I am still having with myself whether it's the part of a dutiful wife to present herself a wiggling sacrifice to science, or whether science should attend to its own business and lead not into temptation the scientifically inclined heads of peaceful households.

You'll say the decision of what was best lay with Jack. Honey, there's the error of your mortal mind! In a question like that my spouse is as one-sided as a Civil War veteran. Say germ-hunt to Jack and it's like dangling a gaudy fly before a hungry carp

I saw Jack off at the station, and went back to the little house. Charity had sent the cook home and with her own hands served all the beloved dainties of my long-ago childhood, trying to coax me into forgetfulness. As you remember, Mate, dinner has always been the happiest hour of the day in our small domain. Now? Well, everything was just the same. The only difference was Jack. And the half circle of bare tablecloth opposite me was about as cheerful as a snowy afternoon at the North Pole. I wandered around the house for awhile, but every time I turned a corner there was a memory waiting to greet me. Now the merriest of them seemed to be covered with a chilly shadow, and every one was pale and ghostly. All night I lay awake, playing at the old game of mental solitaire and keeping tryst with the wind which seemed to tap with unseen fingers at my window and sigh,

> "Then let come what come may
>
> .   .   .   .   .   .
>
> I shall have had my day."

Is it possible, Mate, that my glorious day, which I thought had barely tipped the hour of noon, is already lengthening into the still shadows of evening?

It was foolish but, for the small comfort I got out of it, I turned on the light and looked inside my wedding-ring. Time has worn it a bit but the letters which spell "My Lady of the Decoration," spelled again the old-time thrill into my heart.

What's the use of tying your heart-

strings around a man, and then have
ambition slip the knot and leave you all
a-quiver?

Far be it from me to stand in Jack's
way if germ-stalking is necessary to his
success. Just the same, I could have
spent profitable moments reading the
burial service over every microbe,
home-grown and foreign.

Really, Mate, I've conscientiously
tried every plan Jack proposed and a
few of my own. It was no use. That
day-after-Christmas feeling promptly
suppressed any effort towards content-
ment.

At first there was a certain exhilara-
tion in catching pace with the gay whirl
which for so long had been passed by
for homier things. You will remember
there was a time when the pace of that
same whirl was never swift enough for
me; but my taste for it now was gone,

13

and it was like trying to do a two-step to a funeral march. For once in my life I knew the real meaning of that poor old worn-to-a-frazzle call of the East, for now the dominant note was the call of love.

I heard it above the clink of the tea-cups. It was in the swish of every silk petticoat. If I went to the theater, church or concert, the call of that germ-ridden spot of the unholy name beat into my brain with the persistency of a tom-tom on a Chinese holiday.

Say what you will, Mate, it once took all my courage to leave those I loved best and go to far-away Japan. Now it required more than I could dig up to *stay*—with the best on the other side of the Pacific.

The struggle was easy and swift. The tom-tom won and I am on my way to be next-door neighbor to Jack.

14

The Lady and Sada San

Those whom it concerned here were away from home, so I told no one good-by, thus saving everybody so much wasted advice. If there were a tax on advice the necessities of life would not come so high. Charity followed me to the train, protesting to the last that "Marse Jack gwine doubt her velocity when she tell him de truf bout her lady going a-gaddin' off by herse'f and payin' no mind to her ole mammy's prosterations." I asked her to come with me as maid. She refused; said her church was to have an ice-cream sociable and she had "to fry de fish."

This letter will find you joyfully busy with the babies and the "only man." Blest woman that you are.

But I know you. I have a feeling that you have a few remarks to make. So hurry up. Let us get it off our minds. Then I can better tell you what

15

The Lady and Sada San

I am doing. Something is going to happen. It usually does when I am around. I have been asked to chaperone a young girl whose face and name spell romance. If I were seeking occupation here is the opportunity knocking my door into splinters.

Still at Sea. June, 1911.

Any time you are out of a job and want to overwork all your faculties and a few emotions, try chaperoning a young room-mate answering to the name of Sada San, who is one-half American dash, and the other half the unnamable witchery of a Japanese woman; a girl with the notes of a lark in her voice when she sings to the soft twang of an old guitar.

If, too, you are seeking to study psychological effect of such a combination on people, good, middlin' and oth-

The Lady and Sada San

erwise, I would suggest a Pacific liner
as offering fifty-seven varieties, and
then some.

The last twinge of conscience I had
over coming, died a cheerful death.
I 'd do it again. For not only is romance surcharging the air, but fate
gives promise of weaving an intricate
pattern in the story of this maid whose
life is just fairly begun and whom the
luck of the road has given me as traveling mate. Now, remembering a few
biffs fate has given me, I have no burning desire to meddle with her business.
Neither am I hungering for responsibility. But what are you going to say
to yourself, when a young girl with a
look in her eyes you would wish your
daughter to have, unhesitatingly gives
you a letter addressed at large to some
"Christian Sister"! You read it to
find it 's from her home pastor, re-

questing just a little companionship for "a tender young soul who is trying her wings for the first time in the big and beautiful world"! I have a very private opinion about reading my title clear to the Christian Sister business, but no woman with a heart as big as a pinch of snuff could resist giving her very best and much more to the slip of a winsome maid, who confidingly asks it—especially if the sister has any knowledge of the shadows lurking in the beautiful world.

Mate, these steamers as they sail from shore to shore are like giant theaters. Every trip is an impromptu drama where comedy, farce, and often startling tragedy offer large speaking parts. The revelation of human nature in the original package is funny and pathetic. Amusement is always on

The Lady and Sada San

tap and life stories are just hanging
out of the port-hole waiting to attack
your sympathy or tickle your funny
bone. But you 'd have to travel far to
find the beginning of a story so heaped
up with romantic interest as that of
Sada San as she told it to me, one long,
lazy afternoon as I lay on the couch in
my cabin, thanking my stars I was getting the best of the bare tablecloth and
the empty house at home.

Some twenty years ago Sada's
father, an American, grew tired of the
slow life in a slow town and lent ear to
the fairy stories told of the Far East,
where fortunes were made by looking
wise for a few moments every morning and devoting the rest of the day to
samisens and flutes. He found the
glorious country of Japan. The be-
guiling tea-houses, and softly swinging

sampans were all too distracting. They sang ambition to sleep and the fortune escaped.

He drifted, and at last sought a mean existence as teacher of English in a school of a remote seaside village. His spirit broke when the message came of the death of the girl in America who was waiting for him. Isolation from his kind and bitter hours left for thought made life alone too ghastly. He tried to make it more endurable by taking the pretty daughter of the head man of the village as his wife.

My temperature took a tumble when I saw proofs of a hard and fast marriage ceremony, signed and countersigned by a missionary brother who meant business.

You say it is a sordid tale? Mate, I know a certain spot in this Land of Blossoms, where only foreigners are

laid to rest, which bears testimony to a
hundred of its kind—strange and pitiful destinies begun with high and brilliant hopes in their native land; and
when illusions have faded, the end has
borne the stamp of tragedy, because
suicide proved the open door out of a
life of failure and exile.

Sada's father was saved suicide and
long unhappiness by a timely tidal-
wave, which swept the village nearly
bare, and carried the man and his wife
out to sea and to eternity.

The child was found by Susan West
who came from a neighboring town to
care for the sick and hungry. Susan
was a teacher-missionary. Not much
to look at, if her picture told the truth,
but from bits of her history that I 've
picked up her life was a brighter jewel
than most of us will ever find in a
heavenly crown. Instead of holding the

unbeliever by the nape of the neck and thrusting a not-understood doctrine down his unwilling throat, she lived the simple creed of loving her neighbor better than herself. And the old pair of goggles she wore made little halos around the least speck of good she found in any transgressor, no matter how warped with evil.

When she was n't helping some helpless sinner to see the rainbow of promise at the end of the straight and narrow way, Susan spent her time and all her salary, giving sick babies a fighting chance for life. She took the half-drowned little Sada home with her, and searched for any kinsman left the child. There was only one, her mother's brother. He was very poor and gladly gave his consent that Miss West should keep the child—as long as it was a girl! Susan had taught the man English once in the long ago and this was his chance to repay her.

Later on when the teacher found her health failing and headed for home in America, Uncle Mura was still more generous and raised no objections to her taking the baby with her.

Together they lived in a small Western town. The missionary reared the child by rule of love only and went on short rations to educate her. Sada's eager mind absorbed everything offered her like a young sponge, and when a few months ago Susanna folded her hands and joined her foremothers, there was let loose on the world this exquisite girl with her solitary legacy of untried ideals and a blind enthusiasm for her mother's people.

Right here, Mate, was when I had a prolonged attack of cold shivers. Just before Miss West passed along, knowing that the Valley was near, she wrote to Uncle in Japan and told him that his niece would soon be alone. Can't you imagine the picture she drew of her foster child who had satisfied every craving of her big mother heart? Fascinating and charming and so weighted with possibilities, that Mura, who had prospered, leaped for his chance and sent Sada San money for the passage over.

Not a mite of anxiety shadowed her eyes when she told me that Uncle kept a wonderful tea-house in Kioto. He must be very rich, she thought, because he wrote her of the beautiful things she was to have. About this time the room seemed suffocating. I got up and turned on the electric fan. The only thing required of her, she continued, was to use her voice to entertain Uncle's friends. But she hoped to do much more. Through Miss West she knew how many of her mother's dear people needed help. How glorious that she was young and strong and could give so much. Susan had also talked to her of the flowers, the lovely scenery, the poetry of the people and their splendid spirit—making a dreamland where even man was perfect. How she loved it! How proud she was to feel that in part it was her country. Faithfully would she serve it. Oh, Susanna West! I'd like to shake you till your harp snapped a string. It's like sending a baby to pick flowers on the edge of a bottomless pit.

What could I say! The missionary-teacher had told the truth. She simply failed to mention that in the fairy-land there are cherry-blossom lanes down which no human can wander without being torn by the brier patches.

The Lady and Sada San

The path usually starts from a wonderful tea-house where Uncles have grown rich. Miss West didn't mean to shirk her duty. In most things the begoggled lady was a visionary with a theory that if you don't talk about a thing it does not exist; and like most of her kind she swept the disagreeables into a dust heap and made for the high places where all was lovely. And yet she had toiled with the girl through all the difficulties of the Japanese language; and, to give her a musical education, had pinched to the point of buying one hat in eight years!

Now it is all done and Sada is launched on the high seas of life with a pleasure-house for a home and an unscrupulous Uncle with unlimited authority for a chaperon. Shades of Susan! but I am hoping guardian angels are "really truly," even if invisible.

Good night, Mate. This game of playing tag with jarring thoughts, new and old, has made six extra wrinkles. I am glad I came and you and Jack will have to be, for to quote Charity, "I 'se done resoluted on my word of honah" to keep my hands, if possible, on Sada whose eyes are as blue as her hair is black.

PACIFIC OCEAN.

Since morning the sea has been a sheet of blue, streaked with the silver of flying fish. That is all the scenery there is; not a sail nor a bird nor an insect. Either the unchanging view or something in the air has stimulated everybody into being their nicest. It is surprising how quickly graciousness possesses some people when there is a witching girl around. Vivacious young men and benevolent officers have suddenly appeared out of nowhere, spick and span in white duck and their winningest smiles. Entertainments dovetail till there is barely time for change of costume between acts.

But let me tell you, Mate, living up to being a mother is no idle pastime, particularly if it means reviving the lost art of managing love-smitten youths and elderly male coquettes. There is a specimen of each opposite Sada and me at table who are so generous with their company on deck, before and after meals, I have almost run out of excuses and am short on plans to avoid the heavy obligations of their eager attentions.

The youth is a To-Be-Ruler of many people, a Maharajah of India. But the name is bigger than the man. Two years ago his father started the boy around the world with a sack full of rubles and a head full of ancient Indian lore. With these assets he paused at Oxford that he might skim through the classics. He had been told this was where all the going-to-be-great men stopped to acquire just the proper tone of superiority so necessary in ruling a country. Of course he picked up a bit on electricity, mechanics, etc. This accomplished to his satisfaction he ran over to America to view the barbarians' god of money and take a glance at their houses which touched the sky. But his whole purpose in living, he told me, was to yield himself to certain meditations, so that in his final reincarnation, which was only a few centuries off, he would return to the real thing in Buddha. In the meantime he was to be a lion, a tiger and a little white bird. At present he is plain human, with the world-old malady gnawing at his heart, a pain which threatens to send his cogitations whooping down a thornier and rosier lane than any Buddha ever knew. Besides I am thinking a few worldly vanities have crept in and set him back an eon or so. He wears purple socks, pink ties and a dainty watch strapped around his childish wrist.

When I asked him what impressed him most in America, he promptly answered with his eyes on Sada, "Them girls. They are rapturous!"

Farewell Nirvana! With a camp stool in one hand and a rosary in the other, he follows Sada San like the shadow on a sun dial. Wherever she is seated, there is the stool and the royal youth, his mournful eyes feasting on the curves and dimples of her face, her lightest jest far sweeter than any prayer, the beads in his hand forgotten.

The other would-be swain calls himself a Seeker of Truth. Incidentally he is hunting a wife. His general attitude is a constant reminder of the uncertainty of life. His presence makes you glad that nothing lasts. He says his days are heavy with the problems of the universe, but you can see for yourself that this very commercial traveler carries a light side line in an assortment of flirtations that surely must be like dancing little sunbeams on a life of gloom.

Goodness knows how much of a nuisance he would be if it were not for a little lady named Dolly, who sits beside him, gray in color, dress and experience. At no uncertain age she has found a belated youthfulness and is starting on the first pleasure trip of her life.

Coming across the country to San Francisco, her train was wrecked. In the smash-up a rude chair struck her just south of the belt line and she fears brain fever from the blow. The alarm is not general, for though just freed by kind death from an unhappy life sentence of matrimony she is ready to try another jailer.

Whether he spied Dolly first and hoped that the gleam from her many jewels would light up the path in his search for Truth and a few other things, or whether the Seeker was sought, I do not know. However the flirtation which seems to have no age limit has flourished like a bamboo tree. For once the man was too earnest. Dolly gave heed and promptly attached

32

herself with the persistency of a barnacle to a weather-beaten junk. By devices worthy a finished fisher of men, she holds him to his job of suitor, and if in a moment of abstraction his would-be ardor for Sada grows too perceptible, the little lady reels in a yard or so of line to make sure her prize is still dangling on the hook.

To-day at tiffin the griefless widow unconsciously scored at the expense of the Seeker, to the delight of the whole table. For Sada's benefit this man quoted a long passage from some German philosopher. At least it sounded like that. It was far above the little gray head he was trying to ignore and so weighty I feared for her mentality. But I did not know Dolly. She rose like a doughnut. Looking like a child who delights in the rhythm of meaningless sounds, she heard him through, then exclaimed with breathless delight, "Oh, ain't he fluid?"

The man fled, but not before he had asked Sada for two dances at night.

It is like a funny little curtain-raiser, with jealousy as a gray-haired Cupid. So far as Sada is concerned, it is admiration gone to waste. Even if she were not gaily indifferent, she is too absorbed in the happy days she thinks are awaiting her. Poor child! Little she knows of the limited possibilities of a Japanese girl's life; and what the effect of the painful restrictions will be on one of her rearing, I dare not think.

Once she is under the authority of Uncle, the Prince, the Seeker, and all mankind will be swept into oblivion; and, until such time as she can be married profitably and to her master's liking, she will know no man. The cruelest awakening she will face is the attitude of the Orient toward the innocent offspring in whose veins runs the blood of two races, separated by differences which never have been and never will be overcome.

In America the girl's way would not have been so hard because her novel charm would have carried her far. But *hear me:* in Japan, the very wave in her hair and the color of her eyes will prove a barrier to the highest and best in the land. Even with youth and beauty and intelligence, unqualified recognition for the Eurasian is as rare as a square egg.

Another thought hits me in the face as if suddenly meeting a cross bumble-bee. Will the teachings of the woman, who lived with her head in the clouds, hold hard and fast when Uncle puts on the screws?

The Seeker says it is the fellow who

thinks first that wins. He speaks feelingly on the subject. Right now I am going to begin cultivating first thought, and try to be near if danger, whose name is Uncle, threatens the girl who has walked into my affections and made herself at home.

Later.

All the very good people are in bed. The very worldly minded and the young are on deck reluctantly finishing the last dance under a canopy of make-believe cherry blossoms and wistaria. I am on the deck between, closing this letter to you which I will mail in Yokohama in a few hours.

In a way I shall be glad to see a quiet room in a hotel and hie me back to simple living, free from the responsibilities of a temporary parent. I am not promising myself any gay thrills in the meantime. What's the use, with Jack on the borderland of a sulphurous country and you in the Garden of Eden? His letters and yours will be my greatest excitement. So write and keep on writing and never fear that I will not do the same. You are the safety-valve for my speaking emotions, Mate; so let that help you bear it.

Please mark with red ink one small detail of Sada's story. When I was fastening her simple white gown for the dance her chatter was like that of a sunny-hearted child. Indeed, she liked to dance. Susan did not think it harmful. She said if your heart was right your feet would follow. When Miss West could spare her she always went to parties with *Billy,* and oh, how he could dance if he was so big and had red hair.

So! there was a Billy? I looked in

The Lady and Sada San

her face for signs. The way was clear
but there was a soft little quiver in her
voice that caused me carefully to label
the unknown William, and lay him on
a shelf for future reference. Whatever the coming days hold for her,
mine has been the privilege of giving
the girl three weeks of unclouded happiness.

Outside I hear the little Prince pa-
cing up and down, yielding up his soul
to holy meditations. I 'd be willing to
wager my best piece of jade his con-
templations are something like a cycle
from Nirvana, and closer far to a pair
of heavily fringed eyes. Poor little
imitation Buddha! He is grasping at
the moon's reflection on the water.
Somewhere near I hear Dolly's soft coo
and deep-voiced replies. But unfinished packing, a bath and coffee are
awaiting me.

The Lady and Sada San

Dawn is coming, and already through the port hole I see a dot of earth curled against the horizon. Above floats Fuji, the base wrapped in mists, the peak eternally white, a giant snowdrop swinging in a dome of perfect blue. The vision is a call to prayer, a wooing of the soul to the heights of undimmed splendor.

After all, Mate, I may give you and Jack a glad surprise and justify Sada handing me that letter addressed to a Christian Sister.

YOKOHAMA, July, 1911.

Now that I am here, I am trying to decide what to do with myself. At home each day was so full of happy things and the happiest of all was listening for Jack's merry whistle as he opened the street door every night. At home there are always demands, big and little, popping in on me which I sometimes resent and yet being free from makes me feel as dismal as a long vacant house with the For Rent sign up, looks. In this Lotus land there is no *must* of any kind for the alien, and the only whistles I hear belong to the fierce little tugs that buzz around in the harbor, in and out among the white sails of the fishing fleet like big black beetles in a field of lilies. But you must not think life dull for me. Fate and I have cried a truce, and she is showing me a few hands she is dealing other people. But first listen to the tale I have to tell of the bruise she gave my pride this morning, that will show black for many a day.

I joined a crowd on the water's edge in front of the hotel to watch a funeral procession in boats. Recently a hundred and eighty fishermen were sent to the bottom by a big typhoon, and the wives and the sweethearts were being towed out to sea to pay a last tribute to them, by strewing the fatal spot with flowers and paper prayers. White-robed priests stood up in the front of the boats and chanted some mournful ritual, keeping time to the dull thumping of a drum. The air was heavy with incense. A dreamy melancholy filled the air and I thought how hallowed and beautiful a thing is memory. From out that silent watching crowd came a voice that sent my thoughts flying to starry nights of long ago and my first trip across the Pacific; soft south winds; vows of eternal devotion that kept time with the distant throbbing of a ship's engine. I turned. I was facing little Germany and five littler Germanys strung out behind. You surely remember him? and how when I

could n't see things his way he swore to
a wrecked heart and a never-to-be-forgotten constancy. Mate! There was
no more of a flicker of memory in the
stare of his round blue eyes than there
would have been in a newly baked
pretzel. I stood still, waiting for some
glimmer of recognition. Instead, he
turned to the pincushion on his arm,
whom I took to be Ma G., and I heard
him say "Herzallorliebsten." I went
straight to the hotel and had it trans-
lated. Thought it had a familiar
sound. Would n't it be interesting to
know how many "only ones" any
man's life history records? To think
of my imagining him eating his heart
out with hopeless longing in some far
away Tibetan Monastery. And here he
was, pudgy and content, with his fat
little brood waddling along behind him.
If our vision could penetrate the fu-

ture, verily Romance would have to close up shop. Oh, no! I didn't want him to pine entirely away, but he needn't have been in such an everlasting hurry to get fat and prosperous over it. Wouldn't Jack howl?

I took good care to see that he was not stopping at this hotel. Then I went back to my own thoughts of the happy years that had been mine since Little Germany bade me a tearful good-by.

And, too, I wanted to think out some plan whereby I can keep in touch with Sada and be friendly with her relative.

Before I left the steamer, I had a surprise in the way of Uncles. Next time I will pause before I prophesy. But if Uncle was a blow to my preconceived ideas, I will venture Sada startled a few of his traditions as to nieces. Quarantine inspection was short, and when at last we cast anchor, the harbor

43

was as blue as if a patch of the summer sky had dropped into it. The thatched roofs shone russet brown against the dark foliage of the hills. The temple roofs curved gracefully above the pink mist of the crêpe myrtle.

Sada was standing by me on the upper deck, fascinated by the picture. As she realized the long dreamed-of fairy-land was unfolding before her, tears of joy filled her eyes and tears of another kind filled mine.

Sampans, launches and lighters clustered around the steamer as birds of prey gather to a feast: captains in gilt braid; coolies in blue and white, with their calling-cards stamped in large letters on their backs, and the story of their trade written around the tail of their coats in fantastic Japanese characters. Gentlemen in divided skirts and ladies in kimono and clogs swarmed

up the gangway. In the smiling, push-
ing crowd I looked for the low-browed
relative I expected to see. Imagine the
shock, Mate, when a man with manners
as beautiful as his silk kimono pre-
sented his card and announced that he
was Uncle Mura. I had been pointed
out as Sada's friend. A week afterwards I could have thought of something brilliant to say. Taken un-
awares, I stammered out a hope that
his honorable teeth were well and his
health poor. You see I am all right in
Japanese if I do the talking. For I
know what I want to say and what they
ought to say. But when they come at
me with a flank movement, as it were,
I am lost. Uncle passed over my blun-
der without a smile and went on to say
many remarkable things, if sound
means anything. However, trust even
a deaf woman to prick up her ears when

a compliment is headed her way, whether it is in Sanskrit or Polynesian. In acknowledgment I stuck to my flag, and the man's command of quaint but correct English convinced me that I would have to specialize in something more than first thought if I was to cope with this tea-house proprietor whose armor is the subtle manners of the courtier.

Blessed Sada! Only the cocksureness of youth made her blind to the check her enthusiasm was meant to receive in the first encounter of the new life. She had always met people on equal terms, most men falling easy victims. She was blissfully ignorant that Mura, by directing his conversation to me, meant to convey to her that well-bred girls in this enchanted land lowered their eyes and folded their hands when they talked in the presence of a MAN, if they dared to talk at all.

Not so this half-child of the West. She fairly palpitated with joy and babbled away with the freedom of a sunny brook in the shadow of a grim forest. From the man's standpoint, he was not unkind; unrestraint was to him an incomprehensible factor in a young girl's make-up; and whatever was to follow, the first characters he meant her to learn must spell reverence and repression.

They hurried ashore to catch a train to Kioto. I must look harmless, for I was invited to call. I shall accept, for I have a feeling in spite of manners and silken robes that the day is not distant when the distress signals will be flying.

I waved good-by to the girl as the little launch made its way to land. She made a trumpet of her hands and called a merry "sayonara." The master of her future folded his arms and looked out to sea.

The next day I had a lonely lunch at the hotel. When I saw two lovery young things at the table where Jack and I had our wedding breakfast, so long ago, I made for the other end of the room and persistently turned my back. But I saw out of the corner of my eye they were far away above food, and, Mate, believe me, they did n't even know it was hot, though a rain barrel could n't have measured the humidity.

Of course Jack and I were much more sensible, but that whole blessed time is wrapped in rosy mists with streaks of moonlight to the tune of heavenly music, so it 's futile to try to recall just what did happen. I ought to have gone to another hotel, but the chain of memory was too strong for me.

The Lady and Sada San

I was hesitating between the luxury of a sentimental spell and a fit of loneliness, when a happy interruption came in a message from Countess Otani, naming the next day at two for luncheon with her at the Arsenal Gardens at Tokio. How I wished for you, Mate! It was a fairy-story come true, dragons and all. The Arsenal Garden means just what it says. Only when the dove of peace is on duty are its gates opened, and then to but a few, high in command. For across the white-blossomed hedge that encloses the grounds, armies of men toil ceaselessly molding black bullets for pale people and they work so silently that the birds keep house in the long fringed willows and the goldfish splash in the sunned spots of the tiny lake.

After passing the dragons in the shape of sentries and soldiers, to each of whom I gave a brief life-history, I wisely followed my nose and a guard down the devious path.

The Countess received her guests in a banquet-hall all ebony and gold, and was not seated permanently on a throne with a diamond crown screwed into her head as we used so fondly to imagine.

The simplicity of her hospitality was charming. She and most of her ladies-in-waiting had been educated abroad. But despite the lure of the Western freedom, they had returned to their country with their heads level and their traditions intact. But you guess wrong, honey, if you imagine custom and formality of official life have so overcome these high-born ladies as to make them lay figures who dare not raise their eyes except by rule. There were three American guests, and only

by being as nimble as grasshoppers did
we hold our own in the table talk which
was as exhilarating as a game of snowball on a frosty day.

We scampered all around war and
settled a few important political questions. Poetry, books and the new Cab-
inet vied with the merriment over com-
parisons in styles of dress. One delightful woman told how gloves and
shoes had choked her when she first
wore them in America. Another gave
her experience in getting fatally twisted
in her court train when she was making
her bow before the German Empress.

A soft-voiced matron made us laugh
over her story of how, when she was
a young girl at a mission school, she
unintentionally joined in a Christian
prayer, and nearly took the skin off
her tongue afterwards scrubbing it
with strong soap and water to wash

51

away the stain. There was n't even a smile as she quietly spoke of the many times later when with that same prayer she had tried to make less hard the after-horrors of war.

The possibilities of Japanese women are amazing even to one who thinks he knows them. They look as if made for decoration only, and with a flirt of their sleeves they bring out a surprise that turns your ideas a double somersault. Here they were, laughing and chatting like a bunch of fresh schoolgirls for whom life was one long holiday. Yet ten out of the number had recently packed away their gorgeous clothes, and laid on a high shelf all royal ranks and rights, for a nurse's dress and kit. Apparently delicate and shy they can be, if emergency demands, as grim as war or as tender as heaven.

It was a blithesome day and if it

had n't been for that "all gone" sort of
a feeling, that possesses me when evening draws near and Jack is far away,
content might have marked me as her
own. As it was I put off playing a
single at dinner as long as possible
by calling on a month-old bride whom
I had known as a girl. With glee I
accepted the offer of an automobile to
take me for the visit, and repented later.
Two small chauffeurs and a diminutive
footman raced me through the narrow,
crowded streets, scattering the popu-
lace to any shelter it could find. The
only reason we did n't take the fronts
out of the shops is that Japanese shops
are frontless. I looked back to see
the countless victims of our speed. I
saw only a crowd coming from cover,
smiling with curiosity and interest.
We hit the top of the hill with a flour-
ish, and when I asked what was the

hurry my attendants looked hurt and reproachfully asked if that was n't the way Americans liked to ride.

Mate, this is a land of contrasts and contradictions. At the garden all had been life and color. At this home, where the wrinkled old servitor opened the heavily carved gates for me, it was as if I had stepped into a bit of ancient Japan, jealously guarded from any encroachment of new conditions or change of custom.

Like a curious package, contents unknown, I was passed from one automatic servant to another till I finally reached the *Torishimari* or mistress of ceremonies. By clock-work she offered me a seat on the floor, a fan and congratulations. This last simply because I was me. The house was ancient and beautiful. The room in which I sat had nothing in it but matting as fine as silk,

54

The Lady and Sada San

a rare old vase with two flowers and a leaf in formal arrangement, and an atmosphere of aloofness that lulled mind and body to restful revery. After my capacity for tea and sugared dough was tested, the little serving maid fanning me, bowing every time I blinked, the paper doors near by divided noiselessly and, framed by the dim light, sat the young bride, quaint and oriental as if she had stepped out of some century-old kakemono. In contrast to my recent hostesses it was like coming from a garden of brilliant flowers into the soft, quiet shadows of a bamboo grove. No modern touch about this lady. She had been reduced by rule from a romping girl to a selfless creature fit for a Japanese gentleman's wife and no questions asked. Her hair, her dress, and even her speech were strictly by the laws laid down in a book for the thirty-first day of the first month after marriage. But I would like to see the convention with a crust thick enough to entirely obliterate one woman's interest in another whose clothes and life belong to a distant land. When I told her I had come to Japan against Jack's wishes and was going to follow him to China if I could, she paled at my rashness. How could a woman dare disobey? Would not my husband send me home, take my name off the house register and put somebody in my place?

Well now, wouldn't you like to see the scientist play any such tricks with me—that blessed old Jack who smiles at my follies, asks my advice, and does as he pleases, and for whom there has never been but the one woman in the world! I struggled to make plain to her the attitude of American men and women and the semi-independence of the latter. As well explain theology to a child. To her mind the undeviating path of absolute obedience was the only possible way. Anything outside of a complete renunciation of self-interest and thought meant ruin and was not even to be whispered about. I gave it up and came back to her sphere of poetry and mothers-in-law.

When I said good-by there was a gentle pity in her eyes, for she was certain her long-time friend was headed for the highroad of destruction. But instead I turned into the dim solitude of Shiba Park. I had something to think about. To-day's experiences had painted anew in flaming colors the difference in husbands. How prone a woman is, who is free and dearly beloved, to fall into the habit of taking things for granted, forgetting how one drop of the full measure of happiness,

that a good husband gives her, would
turn to rosy tints the gray lives of hundreds of her kind who are wives in
name only. Her appreciation may be
abundant but it is the silent kind. Her
bugaboo is fear of sentiment and when
it is too late, she remembers with a
heart-break.

I can think of a thousand things right
now I want to say to Jack and while
storing them away for some future
happy hour, I walked further into the
deep shadows of twilight.

Instantly the spell of the East was
over me. Real life was not. In the soft
green silences of mystery and fancy, I
found a seat by an ancient moss-cov-
ered tomb. Dreamily I watched a
great red dragon-fly frivol with the
fairy blue wreaths of incense-smoke
that hovered above the leaf shadows
trembling on the sand. The deep mel-

The Lady and Sada San

ody of a bell, sifted through a cloud of blossom, caught up my willing soul and floated out to sea and Jack far from this lovely land, where stalks unrestrained the ugly skeleton of easy divorce for men. The subject always irritates me like prickly heat.

NIKKO, July, 1911.

Summer in Japan is no joke, especially if you are waiting for letters. I know perfectly well I can't hear from you and Jack for an age, and yet I watch for the postman three times a day, as a hungry man waits for the dinner-bell.

The days in Yokohama were too much like a continuous Turkish bath, and I fled to Nikko, the ever moist and mossy. Two things you can always expect in this village of "roaring, windswept mountains,"—rain and courtesy.

The Lady and Sada San

One is as inevitable as the other, and both are served in quantities.

I am staying in a semi-foreign hotel which is tucked away in a pocket in the side of a mountain as comfy as a fat old lady in a big rocker who glories in dispensing hospitality with both hands. Just let me put my head out of my room door and the hall fairly blossoms with little maids eager to serve. A step toward the entrance brings to life a small army of attendants bending as they come like animated jack-knives on a live wire. One struggles with the mystery of my overshoes, while the Master stands by and begs me to take care of my honorable spirit. As it is the only spirit I possess I heed his advice and bring it back to the hotel to find the entire force standing at attention, ready to receive me. I pass on to my room with a procession of bear-

ers and bearesses strung out behind
me like the tail of a kite, anything
from a tea-tray to the sugar tongs being sufficient excuse for joining the pa-
rade.

When dressing for dinner, if I press
the button, no less than six little picture maids flutter to my door, each begging for the honor of fastening me up
the back. How delighted Jack would
be to assign them this particular
honor for life. Such whispers over
the wonders of a foreign-made dress
as they struggle with the curious fas-
tenings! (They should hear my lord's
fierce language!) Each one takes a
turn till some sort of connection is
made between hook and eye. All is so
earnestly done I dare not laugh or wig-
gle with impatience. I may sail into
dinner with the upper hook in the lower
eye and the middle all askew, but the

service is so graciously given, I would
rather have my dress upside down than
to grumble. Certainly I pay for it. I
tip everything from the proprietor to
the water-pitcher. But the sum is so
disproportionate to the pleasure and
the comfort returned that I smile to
think of the triple price I have paid
elsewhere and the high-nosed conde-
scension I got in return for my money.
Japanese courtesy may be on the sur-
face, but the polish does not easily wear
off and it soothes the nerves just as the
rain cools the air. It goes without saying that I did not arrive in Nikko without a variety of experiences along the
way.

Two hours out from Yokohama, the
train boy came into the coach, and with
a smile as cheerful as if he were saying, "Happy New Year," announced
that there was a washout in front of us

and a landslide at the back of us. Would everybody please rest their honorable bones in the village while a bridge was built and a river filled in. The passengers trailed into a settlement of straw roofs, bamboo poles and acres of white and yellow lilies. I went to a quaint little inn—that was mostly out!—built over a fussy brook; and a pine tree grew right out of the side of the house. My room was furnished with four mats and a poem hung on the wall. When the policeman came in to apologize for the rudeness of the storm in delaying me, the boy who brought my bags had to step outside so that the official would have room to bow properly. I ate my supper of fish-omelet and turnip pickle served in red lacquer bowls, and drank tea out of cups as big as thimbles. Jack says Japanese teacups ought to be forbidden; in a moment of forgetfulness they could so easily slip down with the tea.

It had been many a year since I was so separated from my kind and each hour of isolation makes clearer a thing I've never doubted, but sometimes forget, that the happiest woman is she whose every moment is taken up in being necessary to somebody; and to such, unoccupied minutes are like so many drops of lead. That, with a telegram I read telling of the increasing dangers of the plague in Manchuria, threatened to send me headlong into a spell of anxiety and the old terrible loneliness.

Happily the proprietor and his wife headed it off by asking me if I would be their guest for this evening to see the Bon Matsuri, the beautiful Festival of the Dead. On the thirteenth day of the seventh month, all the departed spirits take a holiday from Nirvana or any

other seaport they happen to be in and
come on a visit to their former homes
to see how it fares with the living.
Poor homesick spirits! Not even
Heaven can compensate for the separa-
tion from beloved country and friends.
As we passed along, the streets were
alight with burning rushes placed at
many doors to guide the spiritual ex-
cursionists. Inside, the people were
praying, shrines were decorated and
children in holiday dress merrily
romped. Why, Mate, it was worth being a ghost just to come back and see
how happy everybody was. For on
this night of nights, cares and sorrows
are doubly locked in a secret place
and the key put carefully away. You
could n't find a coolie so heartless as to
show a shadow of trouble to his ghostly
relatives when they return for so brief
a time to hold happy communion with

the living. He may be hungry, he may be sick, but there is a brave smile of welcome on his lips for the spirits.

The crazy old temple at the foot of the mountain, glorified by a thousand lights and fluttering flags, reaped a harvest of *rins* and *sens* paid to the priests for paper prayers and bamboo flower-holders with which to decorate the graves. The cemetery was on the side of the hill, and every step of the way somebody stopped at a stone marker to fasten a lantern to a small fishing-pole and pin a prayer near by. This was to guide the spirit to his own particular spot.

A breeze as soft as a happy sigh came through the pines and gently rocked the lanterns. The dim figures of the worshipers moved swiftly about, as delighted as children in the shadow-pictures made by the twinkling lights, eagerly seeking out remote spots that no grave might be without its welcoming gleam. A long line of white-robed dancing girls came swaying by with clapping hands to soft-voiced chanting.

I, too, though an alien, was moved with the good-will and kindness that sung through the very air and fearlessly I would have decorated any festive ghost that happened along. I looked to see where I might lay the offering I held in my hand. My hostess plucked my sleeve and pointed to a tiny tombstone under a camellia tree. I went closer and read the English inscription, "Dorothy Dale. Aged 2 years." There was a tradition that once in the long ago a missionary and his wife lived in the village. Through an awful epidemic of cholera they stuck to their posts, nursed and cared for the

people. Their only child was the price
they paid for their constancy. To each
generation the story had been told, and
through all the years faithful watch
had been kept over the little enclosure.
Now it was all a-glimmer with lanterns
shaped like birds and butterflies. I
added my small offering and turned
hotelwards reluctantly.

My ancient host and hostess trotted
along near by, eager to share all their
pathetic little gaieties with me. Their
lives together had about as much real
comradeship as a small brown hen and
a big gray owl, and they had been married sixty years! They had toiled and
grown old together, but that did not
mean that wifey was to walk anywhere
but three feet to the rear, nor to speak
except when her lord and ruler stopped
talking to take a whiff of his pipe.
I tried to walk behind with the old lady

but she threatened to stand in one spot for the rest of the night. Then I vainly coaxed her to walk with me at her husband's side. But her face was so full of genuine horror at such disrespect that I desisted. Think, Mate, of trying to puzzle out the make-up of a nation which for the sake of a long-ago kindness will for years keep a strange baby's grave green and yet whose laws will divorce a woman for disobedience to her husband's mother and where the ancient custom of "women to heel" still holds good.

And this is the land where the Seeker came for the truth!

Sada thinks it paradise and I, as before, am sending to Jack

> A heart of love for thee
> Blown by the summer breezes
> Ten thousand miles of sea.

The Lady and Sada San

July, 1911.

Mate:

There ought to be some kind of capital punishment for the woman who has nothing to do but kill time. It's an occupation that puts crimps in the soul and offers the supreme moment in which the devil may work his rabbit foot. No, I cannot settle down or hustle up to anything until I hear from Jack or you. Very soon I will be reduced to doing the one desperate thing lurking in this corner of the woods, flirting with the solitary male guest, who has a strong halt in his voice and whose knees are not on speaking terms.

Of course it is raining. If the sun gets gay and tries the bluff of being friendly, a heavy giant of a cloud rises promptly up from behind a mountain and puts him out of business. Still, why moan over the dampness? It makes the hills look like great green plush sofa-cushions and the avenues like mossy caves.

I have read till my eyes are crossed and I have written to every human I know. I have watched the giggling little maids patter up to a two-inch shrine and, flinging a word or two to Buddha, use the rest of their time to gossip. And the old lady who washes her vegetables and her clothes in the same baby-lake just outside my window amuses me for at least ten minutes. Then, Mate, for real satisfaction, I must turn to you, whose patience is elastic and enduring. It is one of my big joys that your interest and love are just the same, as in those other days when you packed me off to Japan for the good of my country and myself; and then sent Jack after me. Guess I should have stayed at home, as Jack told me, but I am glad I did not.

The Lady and Sada San

Though it has poured every minute I have been here, there have been bursts of sunshine inside, if not out. The other day my table boy brought me the menu and asked for an explanation of *assorted* fruits. I told him very carefully it meant *mixed, different kinds*. He is a smart lad. He understands my Japanese! He grasped my meaning immediately, and wrote it down in a little book. This morning he came to my room and announced: "Please, Lady, some assorted guests await you in the audience chamber; one Japanese and two American persons."

I have had my first letter from Sada too, simply spilling over with youth and enthusiasm. The girl is stark mad over the fairy-landness of it all. Says her rooms are in Uncle's private house, which is in quite a different part of the garden from the tea-house. (Thank

the Lord for small mercies!) She says
Uncle has given her some beautiful
clothes and is so good to her. I dare
say. He has taken her to see a lovely
old castle and wonderful temple. The
streets are all pictures and the scenery
is glorious! That is true, but the girl
cannot live off scenery any more than a
nightingale can thrive on the scent of
roses. What is coming when the gla-
mour of the scenery wears off and Uncle puts on the pressure of his will?

I have not dared to give her any suggestion of warning. She is deadly
sure of her duty, so enthralled is she
with the thought of service to her
mother's people. If I am to help her,
the shock of disillusionment must come
from some other direction. The *dis-
illusioner* is seldom forgiven. I do not
know what plans are being worked out
behind Uncle's lowered eyelids. But I

The Lady and Sada San

do know his idea of duty does not include keeping such a valuable asset as a bright and beautiful niece hid away for his solitary joy. In fact, he would consider himself a neglectful and altogether unkind relative if he did not marry Sada off to the very best advantage to himself. In the name of all the Orient, what else is there to do with a *girl,* and especially one whose blood is tainted with that of the West?

Well, Mate, my thoughts grew so thick on the subject I nearly suffocated. I went for a walk and ran right into a cavalcade of donkeys, jinrickshas and chairs, headed by the Seeker and Dolly, who has also annexed the little Maharajah.

They had been up to Chuzenji—and Chuzenji I would have you know is lovely enough, with its emerald lake and rainbow mists, to start a man's tongue

to love-making whether he will or not.
And so surely as it is raining, something has happened. Dolly was as gay
as a day-old butterfly and smiled as if
a curly-headed Cupid had tickled her
with a wing-feather. The Seeker was
deadly solemn. Possibly the aftermath of his impetuosity.

Oh, well! there is no telling what
wonders can be worked by incurable
youthfulness and treasures laid up in
a trust company.

The little Prince, with every pocket
and his handkerchief full of small images of Buddha which he was collecting, asked at once for Sada. His heart
was in his eyes, but there is no use tampering with a to-be-incarnation by encouraging worldly thoughts. So I said
I had not seen her since we landed.
They were due on board the *Siberia* in
Yokohama to-night on their way to

China. I waved them good wishes and went on, amused and not a little troubled. Worried over Sada, hungry for Jack, lonesome for you. I passed one of the gorgeous blue, green and yellow gates, at the entrance of a temple. On one side is carved a distorted figure, that looks like a cross between an elephant and a buzzard. It is called "Baku, the eater of evil dreams." My word! but I could furnish him a feast that would give him the fanciest case of indigestion he ever knew!

Mate, you would have to see Nikko, with its majestic cryptomarias, sheltering the red and gold lacquer temples; you would have to feel the mystery of the gray-green avenues, and have its holy silences fall like a benediction upon a restless spirit, to realize what healing for soul and body is in the very

air, to understand why I joyfully loi-
tered for two hours and came back sane
and hungry, but wet as a fish.

Write me about the only man, the
kiddies and your own blessed happy
self.

I agree with Charity. "Ef you want
to spile a valuable wife, tu'n her loose
in a patch of idlesomeness."

STILL AT NIKKO, August, 1911.

You beloved girl, I have heard from
Jack and my heart is singing a rag-
time tune of joy and thanksgiving.
How he laughed at me for being too
foolishly lonesome to stay in America
without him. Oh, these men! Does
he forget he raged once upon a time,
when he was in America without me?
As long as I am here though, he wants
me to have as good a time as possible.

The Lady and Sada San

Do anything I want, and—blessed
trusting man!—buy anything I see that
will fit in the little house at home.

Can you believe it? After a fierce
battle the sun won out this morning,
and even the blind would know by the
dancing feel of the air that it was a
glorious day. At eight o'clock, when
the little maids went up to the shrine,
happy as kittens let out for a romp,
they forgot even to look Buddha-ward
and took up their worship time in playing tag. The old woman who uses the
five-foot lake as the family wash-tub,
brought out all her clothes, the grand-
baby, and the snub-nosed poodle that
wears a red bib, to celebrate the sunshine by a carnival of washing.

I could not stand four walls a minute
longer. I am down in the garden writing you, in a tea-house made with three
fishing-poles and a bunch of straw. It

is covered with pink morning-glories as big as coffee cups.

It has been three weeks since my last letter and I know your interest in Jack and germs is almost as great as mine. Jack has been in Peking. He thinks the revolution of the Chinese against the Manchu Government is going to be something far more serious this time than a flutter of fans and a sputter of shooting-crackers. The long-suffering worm with the head of a dragon is going to turn, and when it does, there will not be a Manchu left to tell the pig tale.

Jack is in Mukden now, where he is about to lose his mind with joy over the prospect of looking straight in the eye—if it has one—this wicked old germ with a new label, and telling it what he thinks. The technical terms he gives are as paralyzing as a Russian name spelled backwards.

The Lady and Sada San

In a day's time this fearful thing wipes out entire families and villages. It has simply ravaged northern Manchuria and the country about. Jack says so deadly are the effects of these germs in the air that if a man walking along the street happens to breathe in one, he is a corpse on the spot before he is through swallowing. The remains are gathered up by men wearing shrouds and net masks, and the peaceful Oriental who was not doing a thing but attending strictly to his own business, is soon reduced to ashes. All because of a pesky microbe with a surplus of energy.

You know perfectly well, Mate, Jack does not speak in this frivolous manner of his beloved work. The interpretation is wholly mine. But I dare not be serious over it. I must push any thought of his danger to the further ends of nowhere.

Jack thinks the native doctors have put up a brave fight, but so far the laugh has been all on the side of the frisky germ.

It blasts everything it touches and is most fastidious. Nobody can blame it for choosing as its nesting-place the little soft furred Siberian marmots, which the Chinese hunt for their skin. If only the hunters could be given a dip in a sulphur vat before they lay them down to sleep in the unspeakable inns with their spoils wrapped around them, the chance for infection would not be so great. Of course the bare suggestion of a bath might prove more fatal than the plague, for oftener than not the hunters are used only as a method of travel by the merry microbe and are immune from the effects. Of course Jack has all sorts of theories as to why this is so. But did you ever see a scientist who did n't have a workable theory for everything from the wrong end of a carpet-tack to the evolution of a June bug?

From the hunters and their spoils the disease spreads and their path southwards can be traced by desolated villages and piles of bones.

Jack tells me he is garbed in a long white robe effect (I hope he won't grow wings), with a good-sized mosquito net on a frame over his head and face. He works in heavy gloves. Mouth and nose being the favorite point of attack, everybody who ventures out wears over this part of the face a curiously shaped shield, whose firm look says, "No admittance here." But all the same, that germ from Siberia is a wily thief and steals lives by the thousands, in spite of all precautions.

Jack is as enthusiastic over the fight against the scourge as a college boy over football. His letter has so many big technical words in it, I had to pay excess postage.

I 've read his letter twice, but to save me I cannot find any suggestion of the remotest possibility of my coming nearer. Yes, I know I said Japan only. But way down in the cellar of my heart I *hoped* he would say nearer.

What a happy day it has been. Here is your letter, just come. The priests up at the temple have asked me to see the ceremony of offering food to the spirits, in the holy of holies.

There is not time for me to add another word to this letter. What a dear you are, to love while you lecture me. What you say is all true. A woman's

place *is* in her home. But just now out
of the East, I 've had a call to play silent partner to science and while it 's
a lonesome sport, at least it 's far more
entertaining than caring for a husband-
less house. Anyhow I am sending you
a hug and a thousand kisses for the
babies.

Shoji Lake, August, 1911.

Mate, think of the loveliest landscape
picture you ever saw, put me in it and
you will know where I am. With some
friends from Honolulu and a darling
old man—observe I say *old!*—from Colorado, we started two days ago, to walk
around the base of Fuji. Everything
went splendidly till a typhoon hit us
amidships and sent us careening, blind,
battered and soaked into this red and
white refuge of a hotel, that clings to
the side of a mountain like a wood-

pecker to a telephone pole. I have seen storms, but the worst I ever saw was a playful summer breeze compared with the magnificent fury of this wind that snapped great trees in two as if they had been young bean-poles, and whipped the usually peaceful lake into raging waves that swept through a gorge and greedily licked up a whole village.

Our path was high up, but right over the water. Sometimes we were crawling on all fours. Mostly we were flying just where the wind listed. If a tree got in our way as we flew, so much the worse for us. It is funny now, but it was not at the time! Seriously, I was in immediate peril of being blown to glory *via* the fierce green foam below. My Colorado Irishman is not only a darling, but a hero. Once I slipped, and stopped rolling only when some faithful pines were too stubborn to let go.

I was many feet below the reach of any arm. In a twinkling, my friend had stripped the kimono off the baggage coolie's back, and made a lasso with which he pulled me up. Then shocked to a standstill by the shortcomings of the coolie's birthday suit, he snatched off his coat and gave it to him, with a dollar. Such a procession of bedraggled and exhausted pleasure-seekers as we were, when three men stood behind our hotel door and opened it just wide enough to haul us in. But hot baths and boiling tea revived us and soon we were as merry as any people can be who have just escaped annihilation.

The typhoon passed as suddenly as it came, and now the world—or at least this part of it—is as glowing and beautiful as if freshly tinted by the Master Hand.

A moment ago I looked up to see my rescuer gazing out of the window. I asked, "How do you feel, Mr. Carson?" His voice trembled when he answered: "Lady, I feel glorified, satisfied and nigh about petrified. Look at that!"

Below lay Shoji, its shimmering waters rimmed with velvety green. Every raindrop on the pines was a prism; the mountain a brocade of blossom. To the right Fuji, the graceful, ever lovely Fuji; capricious as a coquette and bewitching in her mystery, with a thumbnail moon over her peak, like a silver tiara on the head of a proud beauty; at her base the last fleecy clouds of the day, gathered like worshipers at the feet of some holy saint.

The man's face shone. For forty years he had worked at harness-mak-

ing, always with the vision before him
that some day he might take this trip
around the world. He has the soul of
an artist, which has been half starved in
the narrow environment of his small
town life. Cannot you imagine the
mad revel of his soul in this picture-
land?

He is going to Mukden. Of course
I told him all about Jack's work. The
old fellow, he must be all of seventy,
was thrilled. I am going to give him a
letter to Jack. Also to some friends
in Peking; they will be good to him. If
anybody deserves a merry-go-round
sort of a holiday, he does. Think of
sewing on saddles and bridles all these
years, when his heart was withering for
beauty!

I am glad of your eager interest in
Sada. How like you! Never too absorbed in your own life to share other

people's joys and sorrows and festivities.

If your wise head evolves a plan of action, send by wireless, for if I read aright her message received to-day, the time is fast coming when the red lights of danger will be flashing. I will quote: "Last night Uncle asked me to sing to some people who were giving a dinner at the tea-house. I put on my loveliest kimono and a hair-dresser did my hair in the old Japanese style and stuck a red rose at the side. For the first time I went into that beautiful, *beautiful* place my Uncle calls "the Flower Blooming" tea-house. It was more like a fairy palace. How the girls, who live there, laughed at my guitar. They had never seen one before. How they whispered over the color of my eyes. Said they matched my kimono, and they tittered over my

clumsiness in sitting on the floor. But
I forgot everything when the door slid
open and I looked into the most wonderful dream-garden that ever was, and
people everywhere. I finished singing,
there was clapping and loud *banzais*.
I looked up and realized there were *only*
men at this dinner and I never saw so
many bottles in all my life. I felt very
strange and so far away from dear
Susan West. After I had sung once
more I started back to my home. Uncle
met me. I told him I was going to bed.
For the first time he was cross and ordered me back to the play place, where
I was to stay until he came for me.
There never was anything so lovely as
the green and pink garden and the lily-
shaped lights, and the flowers; and
such *pretty* girls who knew just what to
do. But I cannot understand the men
who come here. When dear old Billy"

—than heaven she says *dear* Billy!—
"talks I know just what he means.
But these men use so many words
Susan never taught me, and laugh so
loud when they say them.

"There was one man named Hara
whose clothes were simply gorgeous.
The girls say he is very rich, and a
great friend of Uncle's! He may have
money, but he is not over-burdened
with manners. He can out-stare an
owl."

There was more. But that is enough
to show me Uncle's hand as plainly as
if I were a palmist. If nothing happens to prevent, the man promises to
do what thousands of his kind have
done before: regardless of obstacles
and consequences marry the girl off to
the highest bidder; rid himself of all
responsibility and make a profit at the
same time. From his point of view it

is the only thing to do. He would be the most astonished uncle in Mikado-land if anybody suggested to him that Sada had any rights or feelings in the matter. He would tell you that as Sada's only male relative, custom gave him the right to dispose of her as he saw fit, and custom is law and there is nothing back of *that!*

So far I have played only a thinking part in the drama. But I will not stand by and see the girl, whose very loneliness is a plea, sacrificed without some kind of a struggle to help her. At the present writing I feel about as effective as a February lamb, and every move calls for tact. Wish I had been born with a needle wit instead of a Roman nose! For if Uncle has a glimmer of a suspicion that I would befriend Sada at the cost of his plans, so surely as the river is lost in the sea, Sada would disappear from my world until it was too late for me to lend a hand.

Good-by, Mate. At eventide, as of old, look my way and send me strength from your vast store of calm courage and common sense. The odds are against me, but the god of luck has never yet failed to laugh with me.

September, 1911.

I am in a monastery, Mate, but only temporarily, thank you. It is a blessing to the cause that Fate did not turn me into a monk or a sister or any of those inconvenient things with a restless religion, that wakes you up about 3 A. M. on a wintry dawn to pray shiveringly to a piece of wood, to the tune of a thumping drum. Some morning when the frost was on the cypress that carven image would disappear!

For one time at least I would have a

93

nice fire, and my prayers would not be decorated with icicles.

For two weeks my friends and I have been tramping through picture-book villages and silk-worm country, and over mountain winding ways, sleeping on the floor, sitting on our feet and giving our stomachs surprise parties with hot, cold and lukewarm rice, sea-weed and devil-fish.

It has been one hilarious lark of out-door life, with nothing to pin us to earth but the joy of being a part of so beautiful a world.

The road led us through superb for-ests, over the Bridge of Paradise to Koyo San, whose peak is so far above the mist-wreathed valleys that it scrapes the clouds as they float by. But I want to say right here; Kobo Daishi, who founded this monastery in the distant ages and built a temple to his own virtues, may have been a saint, but he was not much of a gentleman! Else he would not have been so reckless of the legs and necks of the coming generations, as to blaze the trail to his shrine over mountains so steep that our pack-mule coming up could easily have bitten off his own tail if he had so minded.

Later.

This afternoon I must hustle down. I suppose the only way to get down is to roll. Well; anyway I am in a hurry. My mail beat me up the trail and a letter from Sada San begs me to come to Kioto to see her as soon as I can. She only says she needs help and does not know what to do. And blessed be the telegram that winds up from Hiroshima; the school is in urgent need of an assistant at the Kindergarten and they ask me to come. The principal, Miss Look, has gone to America on business, for three months. Hooray! Here is my chance to resign from the "Folded Hands' Society" and do something that is really worth while, as long as I cannot go to my man. How good it will seem once again to be in that dear old mission school, where in the long ago I toiled and laughed and suffered while I waited for Jack.

The prospect of being with the girls and the kiddies again makes me want to do a Highland Fling, even if I am in a monastery with a sad-faced young priest serving me tea and mournful sighs between prayers.

What a flirtatious old world it is after all. It smites you and bruises you, then binds up the hurts by giving you a desire or so of your heart. Just now the desire of my heart is to catch that train for Kioto.

So here goes a prayer, pinned to a shrine, for a body intact as I tread the path that drops straight down the mountain, through the crimson glory of the maples and the blazing yellow of the gingko tree, to the tiny little station far away that looks like a decorated hen-coop.

KIOTO, September, 1911.

Dearest Mate:

I cannot spend a drop of ink in telling you how I got here. How the baggage beast ran away and decorated the mountain shrubbery with my belongings. And how after all my hurry of dropping down from Koyo San, the brakesman forgot to hook our car to the train and started off on a picnic

97

while the engine went merrily on and left us out in the rice-fields. Suffice it to say I landed in a whirl that spun me down to Uncle's house and back to the hotel. And by the way my thoughts are going, for all I know I may be booked to spin on through eternity.

My visit to Sada was so full of things that did not happen. When I reached the house, I sent in my card to Sada. Uncle came gliding in like a soft-footed panther. He did it so quietly that I jumped when I saw him. We took up valuable time repeating polite greetings, as set down on page ten of the Book of Etiquette, in the chapter on Calls Made by Inconvenient Foreigners.

When our countless bows were finished, I asked in my coaxingest voice if I might see Sada. Presently she came in, dressed in Japanese clothes and

98

beautiful even in her pallor. She was changed—sad, and a little drooping. The conflict of her ideals of duty to her mother's people and the real facts in the case, had marked her face with something far deeper than girlish innocence. It was inevitable. But above the evidences of struggle there was a something which said the dead and gone Susan West had left more than a mere memory. Silently I blessed all her kind.

Sada was unfeignedly glad to see me, and I longed to take her in my arms and kiss her. But such a display would have marked me in Uncle's eyes as a dangerous woman with unsuppressed emotions, and unfit for companionship with Sada. I had hoped his Book of Etiquette said, "After this, bow and depart." But my hopes had not a pin-feather to rest on. He stayed

right where he was. All right, old
Uncle, thought I, if stay you will, then
I shall use all a woman's power to be-
guile you and a woman's wit to out-
trick you, so I can make you show your
hand. It is going to be a game with
the girl as the prize. It is also going
to be like playing leap-frog with a por-
cupine. He has cunning and authority
to back him, and I have only my love
for Sada.

For a time I talked at random, directing my whole conversation to him
as the law demands. By accident, or
luck, I learned that the weak point in
his armor of polite reserve was color
prints. Just talk color prints to a col-
lector and you can pick his pocket with
perfect ease.

My knowledge of color prints could
be written on my thumb nail. But I
made a long and dangerous shot, by

The Lady and Sada San

looking wise and asking if he thought Matahei compared favorably with Moronobo as painters of the same era. I choked off a gasp when I said it, for I would have you know that for all I knew, Matahei might have lived in the time of Jacob and Rebecca, and Moronobo a thousand years afterwards. But I guessed right the very first time and Mura San, with a flash of appreciation at my interest, said that my learning was remarkable. It was an untruth and he knew that I knew it, but it was courteous and I looked easy. Then he talked long and delightfully as only lovers of such things can. At least, it would have been delightful had I not been so anxious to see Sada alone. But it was not to be. At least, not then. But mark one for me, Mate: Uncle was so pleased with my keen and hungry interest in color prints and my desire to see his collection, that he invited me to a feast and a dance at the house the next night.

The following evening I could have hugged the person, male or otherwise, who called my dear host away for a few minutes just before the feast began.

Sada told me hurriedly that Uncle had insisted on her singing every night at the tea-house. She had first rebelled, and then flatly refused, for she did not like the girls. She hated what she saw and was afraid of the men. Her master was furiously angry; said he would teach her what obedience meant in this country. He would marry her off right away and be rid of a girl who thought her foreign religion gave her a right to disobey her relatives. She was afraid he would do it, for he had not asked her to go to the tea-house again. Neither had he permitted her to go out of the house. Once she was sick with fear, for she knew Uncle had been in a long consultation with the rich man Hara and he was in such good humor afterwards. But Hara, she learned, had gone away.

She would *not* sing at these dinners again, not if Uncle choked her and what must she do! I saw the man returning but I quickly whispered, "What about Billy?"

Ah, I knew I was right. The rose in her hair was no pinker than her cheeks. If Billy could only have seen her then, I would wager my shoes—and shoes are precious in this country—that her duty to her mother's people would have to take a back seat.

Before Uncle reached us I whispered, "Keep Billy in your heart, Sada. Write him. Tell him." And in the same breath I heartily thanked Uncle for inviting me.

It *was* a feast, Mate—the most picturesque, uneatable feast I ever sat on my doubly honorable feet to consume. There were opal-eyed fish with shaded pink scales, served whole; soft brown eels split up the back and laid on a bed of green moss; soups, thin and thick; lotus root and mountain lily, and raw fish. Each course—and their name was many—was served on a little two-inch-high lacquer table, with everything to match. Sometimes it was gold lacquer, then again green, once red and another black. But it was all a dream of color that shaded in with the little maids who served it; and they, swift, noiseless and pretty, were trained to graceful perfection. The few furnishings of the room were priceless. Uncle sat by in his silken robes, gracious and courteous, surprising me with his knowledge of current events. In the guise of host, he is charming. That is, if only he would not always talk with dropped eyelids, giving the impression that he is half dreaming and is only partly conscious of the world and its follies. And all the time I know perfectly well that he sees everything around him and clean on to the city limits.

Again and again in his talks he referred to his color prints and the years of patience required to collect them. Right then, Mate, I made a vow to study the pesky things as they have seldom been attacked before—even though I never had much use for pictures in which you cannot tell the top side from the bottom, without a label. But then, Jack says, my artistic temperament will never keep me awake at night. Now I decided all at once to make a collection. Heaven knows what I will do with it. But Uncle grew so enthusiastic he included his niece in the conversation, and while his humor was at high tide I coaxed him into a promise that Sada might come down to Hiroshima very soon, and help me look for prints.

Yes, indeed there was a dance afterwards, and everything was deadly, hysterically solemn—so rigidly proper, so stiffly conventional that it palled. It was the most maleless house of revelry I ever saw. Why, even the kakemono were pictures of perfect ladies and the gate-man was a withered old woman.

There was absolutely nothing wrong I could name. It was all exquisitely, daintily, lawfully Japanese. But I sat by my window till early morning.

The Lady and Sada San

There was a very ghost of a summer moon. Out of the night came the velvety tones of a mighty bell; the singsong prayers of many priests; the rippling laugh of a little child and the tinkling of a samisen. Every sound made for simple joy and peace. But I thought of the girl somewhere beyond the twinkling street lights, who, with mixed races in her blood and a strange religion in her heart, had dreamed dreams of this as a perfect land, and was now paying the price of disillusionment with bitter tears.

Eight o'clock the next morning.

I cabled Jack, "Hiroshima for winter."

He answered, "Thank the Lord you are nailed down at last."

P. S.—I have bought all the books on color prints I could find.

The Lady and Sada San

October, 1911.

Hiroshima! Get up and salute, Mate! Is not that name like the face of an old familiar friend? I have to shake myself to realize that it is not the long ago, but *now*. A recent picture of Jack and one of you and the babies is about the only touch of the present. Everything is just as it was in the old days, when the difficulties of teaching in a foreign kindergarten in a *foreigner* language was the least of the battle that faced me. Well, I thought I'd finished with battles, but there's a feeling of fight in the air.

Same little room, in the same old mission school. Same wall paper, so blue it turned green. And, Lord love us, from the music-rooms still come the sounds like all the harmonies of a baby organ-factory gone on a strike.

But bless you, honey, there is an

eternity of difference in having to stand a thing and doing it of your own free will. As Black Charity would remark, "I don't pay 'em no mind," and let them wheeze out their mournful complaints to the same old hymns.

Had you been here the night my dinky little train pulled into the station, you would have guessed that it was a big Fourth of July celebration or the Emperor's birthday. I would not dare guess how many girls there were to meet me. It seemed like half a mile of them lined up on the platform, and each carried a round red lantern.

Until they had made the proper bow with deadly precision, there was not a smile or a sound. That ceremony over, they charged down upon me in an avalanche of gaiety. They waved their lanterns, they called *banzai*, they laughed and sung some of the old time

109

foolish songs we used to sing. They promptly put to rout all legends of their excessive modesty and shyness. They were just young and girlish. Plain happy. Eager and sweet in their generous welcome. It warmed every fiber of my being. When they thinned out a little, I saw at the other end of the platform a figure flying towards me, with the sleeves of her kimono outstretched like the wings of a gray bird, and a great red rose for a top-knot. It was Miss First River, a little late, but more than happy, as she sobbed out her welcome on the front of my clean shirt-waist.

It was she, you remember, who in all those other years was my faithful secretary and general comforter. The one who slept across my door when I was ill and who never forgot the hot water bag on a cold night. For years she has

supported a drunken father and a crazy
mother; has sent one brother to America and made a preacher of another.

Now she is to be married, she told me
in a little note she slipped into my hand
as we walked up the Street of the Upper Flowing River to the school, adding,
"Please guess my heart."

And miracle of the East! She has
known the man a long time and they
are in love! I am so glad I am going
to be here for the wedding. It comes
off in a few weeks.

I started work in the kindergarten
this morning. It has been said that
when the Lord ran out of mothers
he made kindergartners. Surely he
never did a better job—for the kindergartners. Mate, when I stepped into
that room, it was like going into an enchanted garden of morning-glories and
dahlias. What a greeting the regiment

111

of young Japlings gave me! I just drank in all the fragrance of joy in the eager comradeship and sweet friendliness of the small Mikados and Mikadoesses with a keen delight that made the hours spin like minutes.

And would you believe it? The first sound that greeted my ears after their whole duty had been accomplished in the very formal bow, was—"Oh—it is the *skitten Sensei* (skipping teacher) A skit! A skit! We want to skit!" Of course, they were not the same children by many years. But things die slowly in Hiroshima. Even good reputations. Everything was pushed aside, and work or no work, teachers and children celebrated by one mad revel of skipping.

There are many things to do, and getting into the old harness of steady routine work and living on the tap of

a bell, is not so easy as it sounds, after
years of live-as-you-please. But it is
good for the constitution and is satisfying to the soul.

I once asked my friend Carson from
Colorado if he could choose but one gift
in all the world, what would it be?
"The contintment of stidy work," answered the wise old philosopher from
out of the West; and my heart echoes
his wisdom.

Had a big fat letter from Jack, and
the reputation he gives those germs he
is associating with, is simply disgrace-
ful. He gives me statistics also. Wish
he would n't. It takes so much time
and I always have to count on my fingers.

He tells me, too, of an English woman
who has joined the insect expedition.
Says she is the most brilliant woman
he ever met. Thanks awfully. And

he has to sit up nights studying, to keep up with her. I dare say.

I 'll wager she 's high of color and mighty of muscle and with equal vehemence says a thing is "strawdn'ry" whether it 's a dewdrop or a spouting volcano.

I can't help feeling a little bit envious of her—out there with my Jack! Well! I will not get agitated till I have to.

A note from Sada says Uncle has had another outburst. He still consents for her to come down here. Her beautiful ideals have been smashed to smithereens, and the fact that nothing has ever been invented that will stick them together, adds no comfort to the situation. Her disappointment is heart-breaking. I cannot make a move till I get her to myself and have a life-and-death talk with her. I am playing for time.

The Lady and Sada San

I wrote her a cheerfully foolish letter. Told her I was making all kinds of plans for her visit. I also looked up some doubtful dates—at least, my textbook on color prints said they were doubtful—and referred them to Uncle for confirmation, asking that he give instructions to Sada about a certain dealer in Hiroshima who has some pictures so violent, positively I would not hang them in the cow-shed. That is, if I cared for Suky. But it is anything for conversation now.

I almost forgot to tell you that we have the same *chef* as when I was kindergarten teacher here in the school years ago. He's prosperous as a pawnbroker. He gave me a radiant greeting. "How are you, *Tanaka?*" quoth I. "All same like damn monkey, *Sensei*," he replied. But he is unfailingly cheerful and the cleverest grafter

115

in the universe, with an artistic temperament highly developed; he sometimes
sends in the unchewable roast smoth-
ered in cherry blossoms.

How wise you were, Mate, to choose
home and husband instead of a career.
I love you for it.

HIROSHIMA, October, 1911.

For springing surprises, all full of
kindness and delicate courtesies, Japanese girls would be difficult to equal.
Before a whisper of it reached me, they
made arrangements the other day for
a re-union of all my graduates of the
kindergarten normal class. It is hard
to imagine when they found the time
for the elaborate decorations they put
up in the big kindergarten room, and
the hundred and one little things they
had done to show their love and warmth
of welcome. It was a part of their play

116

to blindfold me and lead me in. When I opened my eyes, there they stood. Twenty-five happy faces smiling into mine, and twenty babies to match. It was the kiddies that saved the day. I was not a little bewildered, and tears stung my eyes. But with one accord the babies set up a howl at anything so inconceivable as a queer foreign thing with a tan head appearing in their midst. When peace was restored by natural methods, the fun began.

The girls fairly bombarded me with questions. Could I come to see every one of them? Where was Jack? Could they see his picture? Did he say I could come? How "glad" it was to be together again. Did I remember how we used to play? Then everybody giggled. One thought had touched them all. Why not play now!

The baby question was quickly settled. Soon there was a roaring fire in my study. We raided the classroom for rugs and cushions and with the collection made down beds in a half ring around the crackling flames. On each we put a baby, feet fireward. We called in the *Obasan* (old woman) to play nurse, and on the table near we placed a row of bottles marked "First aid to the hungry." As I closed the door of the emergency nursery, I looked back to see a semi-circle of pink heels waving hilariously. Surely the fire goddess never had lovelier devotees than the Oriental cherubs that lay cooing and kicking before it that day.

How we played! In all the flowery kingdom so many foolish people could not have been found in one place. What chaff and banter! What laying aside of cares, responsibilities, and heavy hearts, if there were any, and just being

free and young! For a time at least
the years fell away from us and we
relived all the games and folk-dances
we ever knew. True, time had stiff-
ened joints and some of the movements
were about as graceful as a pair of fire
tongs and I may be dismissed for some
of the fancy steps I showed the girls,
but they were happy, and far more sup-
ple than when we began.

When we were breathless we hauled
in our old friend the big *hibachi,* with
a peck of glowing charcoal right in the
middle. We sat on our folded feet and
made a big circle all around, with only
the glimmer of the coals for a light.
Then we talked.

Each girl had a story to tell, either of
herself or some one we had known together. Over many we laughed. For
others the tears started.

Warmed by companionship and

moved by unwonted freedom, how much
the usually reserved women revealed
of themselves, their lives, their trials
and desires! But whatever the story,
the dominant note was acceptance of
what was, without protest. It may be
fatalism, Mate, but it is indisputable
that looking finality in the face had
brought to all of them a quietness of
spirit that no longing for wider fields
or personal ambition can disturb.

None of them had known their husbands before marriage. Few had ever
seen them. Many were compelled to
live with the difficulties of an exacting
mother-in-law, who had forgotten that
she was ever a young wife.

But above it all there was a cheerful
peacefulness; a willingness of service
to the husband and all his demands, a
joy in children and home, that was con-
vincing as to the depth and dignity of

character which can so efface itself for the happiness of others.

One girl, Miss Deserted Lobster Field, was missing. I asked about her and this is her story. She was quite pretty; when she left school there was no difficulty in marrying her off. Two months afterward the young husband left to serve his time in the army. For some reason the mother-in-law did not "enter into the spirit of the girl," and without consulting those most concerned, she divorced her son and sent the girl home. When the soldier-husband returned, a new wife, whom he had never seen, was waiting for him at the cottage door.

The sent-home wife was terribly in the way in her father's house, for by law she belonged neither there nor in any other place. It is difficult to re-marry these offcasts. Something, however, had to be done. So dear father took a stroll out into the village, and being sonless adopted a young boy as the head of his house. A *yoshi* this boy is called. Father married the adopted son to the soldier's wife that was, securely and permanently. A yoshi has no voice in any family matter and is powerless to get a divorce.

Moral: If in Japan you want to make sure of keeping a husband when you get him, take a boy to raise, then marry him.

But the wedding of weddings is the one which took place last summer, by suggestion. The great unseen has lived in America for two years. The maid makes her home in the school. The groom-to-be wrote to a friend in Hiroshima: "Find me a wife." The friend wrote back: "Here she is." Miss Chestnut Tree, the maid, fluttered down to the court-house, had her name put on the house register of the far-away groom, did up her hair as a married woman should and went back to work.

To-morrow she sails for America, and we are all going down to wave her good-by and good luck.

She is married all right. There will be no further ceremony.

I would not dare tell you all the stories they told me. For I would never stop writing and you would never stop laughing or crying.

The end of all things comes sometimes. The beautiful afternoon ended too soon. But for the rest of time, this day will be crowned with halos made with the mightiness of the love and the dearness of the girls who were once my students, always my friends.

It took some time to assort the babies

and make sure of tying the right one on the right mother's back. Not by one shaved head could I see the slightest difference in any of them, but mothers have the knack of knowing.

Out of the big gate they went and down the street all aglow with the early evening lights twinkling in the purple shadows. Their *geta* click-clacked against the hard street, to the music of their voices as they called back to me, *"Oyasumi, Oyasumi, Go kigen yoro shiku"* (Honorably rest. Be happy always to yourself).

My gratitude to this little country is great, Mate. It has given me much. It was here life taught me her sternest lessons. And here I found the heart's-ease of Jack's love. But for nothing am I more thankful than for the love and friendship of the young girl-mothers who were my pupils, but from

124

whom I have learned more of the sweetness and patience of life than I could ever teach.

November, 1911.

Mate, there is a man in Hiroshima for whom I long and watch as I do for no other inhabitant. It is the postman. You should see him grin as he trots around the corner and finds me waiting at the gate, just as I used to do in the old teaching days. I doubly blest him this morning. Thank you for your letter. It fairly sings content. Homeyness is in every pen stroke.

Please say to your small son David that I will give his love to the "king's little boy" *if* I see him. My last glimpse of him was in Nikko. Poor little chap. He was permitted to walk for a moment. In that moment he spied a bantam hen, the anxious mother of half a dozen puff-ball chickens. Royalty knew no denial and went in pursuit. The bantam knew no royalty, pursued also. The four men and six women attendants were in a panic. The baby was rescued from a storm of feathers and taken back to the palace with an extra guard of three policemen.

I have been very busy, at play and at work. We have just had a wedding tea. My former secretary, Miss First River, as she expressed it, "married with" Mr. East Village.

The wedding took place at the ugly little mission church, which was transformed into a beautiful garden, with weeping willows, chrysanthemums, and mountain ferns. Also we had a wedding-bell. In a wild moment of enthusiasm I proposed it. It is always a guess where your enthusiasm will land you out here. I coaxed a cross old tin-

126

ner to make the frame for me. He expostulated the while that the thing was impossible, because it had never been done before in this part of the country. It was rather a weird shape, but I left the girls to trim it and went to the church to help decorate. The bell was to follow upon completion. It failed to follow and after waiting an hour or so I sent for it. The girls came carrying one trimmed bell and one half covered. I asked, "Why are you making two wedding-bells?" My answer was, "Why Sensei! must not the groom have one for his head too?"

Everybody wanted to do something for the little maid, for she had so bravely struggled with adversity of fortune and perversity of family. So there were four flower girls, and the music teacher played *at* the wedding march! In spite of her efforts, Lohen-

The Lady and Sada San

grin seemed suffering as it came from the complaining organ.

Miss First River was a lovely enough picture, in her bridal robes of crêpe, to cause the guests to draw in long breaths of admiration, till the room sounded like the coming of a young cyclone. They were not accustomed to such prominence given a bride, nor to weddings served in Western style.

Oh, yes, the groom was there, a secondary consideration for the first time in the history of Hiroshima, but so in love he did not seem to mind the obscurity.

The ceremony over, the newly-wed seated themselves on a bench facing the guests. An elder of the church arose and with a solemnity befitting a burial, read a sermon on domestic happiness and some forty or fifty congratulatory

128

telegrams. After an hour or so of this and several speeches, cake was passed around, and it was over. At the maid's request I gave her an "American watch with a good engine in it" and my blessing with much love in it, and went back to work. Do not for a minute imagine that because I am not a regularly ordained missionary-sister, that I am not working. The fact is, Mate, the missionaries are still afflicted with the work habit, and so subtle is its cheerful influence, it weaves a spell over all who come near. No matter what your private belief is, you roll up your sleeves and pitch right in when you see them at it, and you put all your heart in it and thank the Lord for the opportunity to help.

The fun begins at 5:30 in the morning, to the merry clang of a brazen bell, and it keeps right on till 6 P. M. For fear of getting rusty before sunrise, some of the teachers have classes at night. I would rather have rest. I am too tired, then, to think.

I have put away all my vanity clothes. No need for them in Hiroshima and in an icy room on a winter's morning, I do not stop to think whether my dress has an in-curve or an out-sweep. I fall into the first thing I find and finish buttoning it when the family fire in the dining-room is reached. A solitary warming-spot to a big house is one of the luxuries of missionary life.

In between times I 've been cheering up the home sickest young Swede that ever got loose from his native heath. So firmly did he believe that Japan was a land where necessity for work doth not corrupt nor the thief of pleasure break through and steal, he gave up a

good position at home and signed a
three-years' contract with an oil firm.
Now he is so sorry, all the pink has
gone out of his cheeks. Until he grows
used to the thought that living where
the Sun flag floats is not a continuous
holiday, the teachers here at school take
turns in making life livable for him.

His entertainment means tramps of
miles into the country, sails on the
lovely Ujina Bay and climbs over the
mountains. In the afternoon the boy
is so in evidence, we almost fall over
him if we step. Yesterday in desperation I tied an apron on him and let
him help me make a cake. Even at
that, with a dab of chocolate on his
cheek and flour on his nose, his summer
sky eyes were weepy whenever he spoke
of his "Mutter." I have done everything for him except lend him my shoul-

der to weep on. It may come to that. There is hope, however. One of our teachers is young and pretty.

Jack, in a much delayed epistle, tells me thrilling and awful things about the plague; says he walks through what was once a prosperous village, and now there is not a live dog to wag a friendly tail. Every house and hovel tenantless. Often unfinished meals on the table and beds just as the occupants left them. A great pit near by full of ashes and bones tells the story of the plague come to town, leaving silent, empty houses, and the dust-laden winds as the only mourners.

The native doctors gave a splendid banquet the other night. With the visiting doctors in full array of evening dress and decorations, Jack says it looked like a big international flag draped around the table. Everybody made a speech and Jack has not stopped yet shooting off fireworks in honor of that Englishwoman.

Well, maybe *I* should have studied science. It is too late now. Besides, I have Uncle on my hands, and I have to commit to memory pages on color printing that run like this: "Fine as a single hair or swelling imperceptibly till it becomes a broken play of light and shade or a mass of solid black, it still flows, unworried and without hesitation on its appointed course."

Sada San is coming down next week. I am looking forward to it with great delight and hunting for a plan whereby I can help her.

Suppose Uncle should give me a glad surprise and come too!

133

The Lady and Sada San

My dear Best Girl:

If ever a sailor needed a compass, I need the level head that tops your loving heart. I am worried hollow-eyed and as useless as a brass turtle.

It has been days since I heard from Jack. When he last wrote, he was going to some remote district out from Mukden. I dare not think what might happen to him. Says he must travel to the very source of the trouble.

If Jack really wanted trouble he could find it nearer home. Is n't it like him, though, with his German education, to hunt a thing to its lair? I suppose when next I hear from him, he will have disappeared into some marmot hole at the foot of a tree in a Siberian forest.

Sada is here. A pale shadow of her former radiant self. She is in deadly

134

fear of what Uncle has written he expects of her when she returns.

For the first few days of her visit, she was like an escaped prisoner. She played and sang with the girls. The joy of her laughter was contagious. Everybody fell a victim to her gaiety. We have been on picnics up the river in a sampan where we waded and fished, then landed on an island of bamboo and fern and cooked our dinner over a *hibachi*. We have had concerts, tableaux and charades, here at the school, with a big table for the stage and a silver moon and a green mosquito-net for the scenery.

In every pastime or pleasure, Sada San has been the moving spirit. Adorably girlish and winning in her innocent joy, I grow faint to think of the rude awakening.

She has talked much of Miss West

and their life together; their work and simple pleasures.

To the older woman she poured out unmeasured affection, fresh and sweet. Susan made a flower garden of the girl's heart, where, if even a tiny weed sprouted it was coaxed into a blossom. But she gave no warning of the savage storms that might come and lay the garden waste.

Well, I'm holding a prayer-meeting a minute that the rosy ideals of the visionary teacher will hold fast when the wind begins to blow.

I found Sada one day on the bed, a crumpled heap of woe; white and shaking with tearless sobs. Anxious to shield her from the persistent friendliness of the girls, I persuaded her to come with me to the old Prince's garden, just back of the school.

She had heard from Uncle. For the

first time he definitely stated his plans.
Hara, the rich man, had sent to him a
proposal of marriage for Sada! Of
course, said Uncle, such an offer from
so prosperous and prominent a man
must be accepted without hesitation.
It was wonderful luck for any girl, said
dear Mura, especially one of her birth.
Nothing further would be done until
she returned, and he wished that to be
at once.

Not a suggestion of feeling or sentiment; not a word as to Sada's wishes
or rights. If these were mentioned to
him, he would undoubtedly reply that
the rights in the matter were all his.
As to feelings, a young girl had no business with such things. His voice would
be courteous, his manner of saying it
would fairly puncture the air.

His letter was simply a cold business
statement for the sale of the girl.

137

The Lady and Sada San

When I looked at the misery in her young eyes, I could joyfully have throttled him and stamped upon him. I wished for a dentist's grinding machine and the chance to bore a nice big hole into each one of his white, even teeth.

She knows nothing of the man Hara except that he is coarse and drinks heavily. The girls in the tea-house always seemed afraid when he came. Vague whispers of his awful life had come to her. What was she to do? She had no money, no place to go, and Uncle was the only relative she had in the world.

Mate, I heard a missionary speak a profound truth, when he said that no Japanese would ever be worth while till all his relatives were dead. Their power is a chain forged around individual freedom.

The Lady and Sada San

She had such loving thoughts of Uncle, Sada sobbed, before she came. She longed to make his home happy and be one of his people. She loved the beautiful country of her mother and craved its friendship.

Miss West had drilled it into her conscience that marriage was holy, and impossible without love. (Bless you, Susan!) She wanted to do her duty, but she *could not* marry this man whom she had never seen but once, and had never spoken to.

She knew the absolute power the law of the land gave Uncle over her. She knew the uselessness of a Japanese girl struggling against the rigid rules laid down by her elders. She knew resistance might bring punishment. Well, Mate, I do not care ever to see again such a look as was in Sada's eyes as she turned her set face to me and forced through her stiff lips a stony, "I won't!" But I thanked God for all the Susan Wests and their teachings.

In spite of the girl's unhappiness, there was a thrill in the region of my heart. Of her own free will Sada San had decided. Now there was something definite to work upon. In the back of my brain a plan was beginning to form. Hope glimmered like a Jack-o'-lantern.

It was late evening. A flaming sunset flushed the sky and bathed the ancient garden of arched bridges and twisted trees in a pinkish haze. The very shadows spelled romance and poetry. It was wise to use the charm of the hour for the beginning of my plan.

I drew Sada down beside me, as we sat in a queer little play-house by the garden lake.

The Lady and Sada San

In olden times it had been the rest place of the Prince Asano, when he was specially moved to write poetry to the moon as it floated up, a silver ball in a navy-blue sky over "Three Umbrella Mountain." Had his ghost been strolling along then, it would have found deeper things than, "in the sadness of the moon night beholds the fading blossom of the heart," to fill his thoughts.

I led the girl to tell me much of her life in Nebraska; of her friends and their amusements. Hers had been the usual story of any fresh wholesome girl. The social life in a small town had limited her experiences, but had kept her deliciously naïve and sweet.

For the first time in our talks, she avoided Billy's name. I hailed it as a beautiful sign. I mentioned William myself and delighted in her red-cheeked confusion. I gently asked her to tell me of him.

She and Billy had gone to school together, played together and he always seemed like a big brother to her. Once a boy had called her a half-breed and Billy promptly knocked him down and sat on his head while he manipulated a shingle.

Another time when they were quite small, the desire of her heart was to ride on the tricycle of a rich little boy who lived across the street. But the pampered youth jeered at her pleadings and exultingly rode up and down before her. Billy saw and bided his time till the small Crœsus was alone. He nabbed him, chucked him in a chicken-coop and stood guard for an hour while Sada rode gloriously.

Through college they were comrades and rivals. Billy had to work his way, for he was the poor son of an invalid mother. From college he had gone straight to a firm of rich manufacturers and was now one of the big buyers.

He had pleaded with her not to come to Japan. He loved her. He wanted her. When she had persisted, he was furious and they had quarreled. But she had thought she was right, then; she did not know how dear Billy was, how big and splendid. She had written to him but seldom, nothing of her disappointment. Maybe he had married. She could not write now. It would be too much like begging, when she was at bay, for the love she had refused when all was well. No, she *could not* tell him.

We talked long and earnestly in that old garden, and the wind that sifted through the pine-needles and the waxy leaves was as gentle as if the spirit of

The Lady and Sada San

Susan West had come to watch and to bless.

I gained a half promise from her that she would write to Billy at once, but I did n't stop there.

Unsuspected by Sada I learned his full address, and Mate, I wrote a letter to the auburn-haired lover in Nebraska, in which I painted a picture that is going to cause something to happen, else I am mistaken in my estimate of the spirit of the West in general and William Weston Milton in particular.

I told him if he loved the girl to come as fast as steam would bring him; that I would help him at the risk of anything, though I have no idea how. I have just returned from a solitary promenade to the post-office through the dark and lonely streets, so that letter will catch to-morrow's American mail.

The Lady and Sada San

Sada told me that for some reason she had never mentioned Billy's name to Uncle. Now isn't that a full hand nestling up my half-sleeve? Uncle thinks the way clear as an empty race-track, and all he has to do is to saunter down the home stretch and gather in the prize-money.

Any scruple on the girl's part will be relentlessly and carelessly brushed aside as a bothersome insect. If she persists, there is always force. He fears nothing from me. I am a for-eigner—from his standpoint too crudely frank to be clever.

He doubtless argues, if he gives it any thought, that if I could I would not dare interfere. And then I am so absorbed in color-prints! So I am, and, I pray Heaven, in some way to his un-doing. The child has no other friend. Shrinkingly she told me of her one attempt to make friends with some high-class people, and the uncompromising rebuff she had received upon their discovering she was an Eurasian. The pure aristocrats seldom lower the social bars to those of mixed blood. I wonder, Mate, if the ghost of failure, who was her father, could see the inheritance of inevitable suffering he has left his child, what his message would be to those who would recklessly dare a like marriage?

Sada goes to Kioto in the morning. She promises not to show resistance, but to keep quiet and alert, writing me at every opportunity.

I am sure Uncle's delight in securing so rich a prize as Hara will burst forth in a big wedding-feast and many rich clothes for the trousseau. I hope so. Preparation will take time. I would rather gain time than treasure.

146

The Lady and Sada San

I put Sada to bed. Tucked her in
and cuddled her to sleep as if she had
been my own daughter.

There she lies now. Her face start-
lingly white against the mass of black
hair. The only sign of her troubled
day is a frequent half-sob and the sadness of her mouth, which is constantly
reading the riot act to her laughing
eyes in the waking hours.

Poor girl! She is only one of many
whose hopes wither like rose-leaves in
a hot sun when met by authority in the
form of tyrannical relatives.

The arched sky over the mountain of
"Two Leaves" is all a-shimmer with
the coming day. Thatched roof and
bamboo grove are daintily etched
against the amber dawn. Lights begin
to twinkle and thrifty tradesmen cheerfully call their wares.

It is a land of peace, a country and

people of wondrous charm; but incomprehensible is the spirit of some of the laws that rule its daughters.

Mate dear:

One of my girls, when attacked with the blues, invariably says in her written apology for a poor lesson, "Please excuse my frivolous with your imagination, for my heart is warmly." So say I.

I am sending you the crêpes and the kimono you asked for. Write for something else. I want an excuse to spend another afternoon in the two-by-four shop, with a play-garden attached, that should be under a glass case in a jewelry store. The proprietor gives me a tea-party and tells me a few of his troubles every time I go to his store. Formerly he kept two shops exclusively for hair ornaments and ribbons.

The Lady and Sada San

He did a thriving trade with school-girls. Recently an order went out from the mighty maker of school laws to the effect that lassies, high and low, must not indulge in such foolish extravagances as head ornaments. The ribbon market went to smash. The old man could not give his stock away. He stored his goods and went to selling high-priced crêpes, which everybody was permitted to wear. Make another request quickly. I would rather shop than think.

Also, if you need any information as to how to run a cooking-school, I will enclose it with the next package.

Since the war, scores of Japanese women are wild to learn foreign cooking. On inquiry as to the reason of such enthusiasm, we found it was because their husbands, while away from home, had acquired a taste for Occi-

The Lady and Sada San

dental dainties. Now their wives want
to know all about them so they can set
up opposition in their homes to the
many tea-houses which offer European
food as an extra attraction. And de-
pend upon it, if the women start to
learn, they stick to it till there is nothing more to know on the subject.

I was to furnish the knowledge and
the ladies the necessary utensils, but I
guess I forgot to mention everything
we might need.

The first thing we tried was biscuit.
All went well until the time came for
baking. I asked for a pan. A pan?
What kind of a pan? Would a wash
pan do? No, if it was all the same I
would rather have a flat pan with a rim.
Certainly! Here it was with a rim and
a handle! A shiny dust-pan greeted
my eyes. Well, there was not very

much difference in the taste of the biscuit.

The prize accomplishment so far has been pies. Our skill has not only brought us fame, but the city is in the throes of a pie epidemic. A few days ago when the old Prince of the Ken came to visit his Hiroshima home, the cooking-ladies, after a few days' consultation, decided that in no better way could royalty be welcomed than by sending him a lemon pie. They sent two creamy affairs elaborately decorated with meringued Fujis. They were the hit of the season. The old gentleman wrote a poem about them saying he ate one and was keeping the other to take back to his country home when he returned a month hence. Then he sent us all a present.

The Lady and Sada San

We have had only one catastrophe. In a moment of reckless adventure my pupils tried a pound cake without a recipe. A pound cake can be nothing else but what it says. That meant a pound of everything and Japanese soda is doubly strong. That was a week ago and we have not been able to stay in the room since.

Good-by! The tailless pink cat and the purple fish with the pale blue eyes are for the kiddies.

I am inclosing an original recipe sent in by Miss Turtle Swamp of Clear Water Village:

Cake.

1 cup of *Desecrated* coconut
5 cup flowers
1 small spoon and barmilla [vanilla]
3 eggs skinned and whipped
1 cup sugar
Stir and pat in pan to cook.

The Lady and Sada San

Mate:

I would be ashamed to tell you how long it is between Jack's letters. He says the activity of the revolutionists in China is seriously interfering with traffic of every kind. All right, let it go at that! Now he has gone way up north of Harbin. In the name of anything *why* cannot he be satisfied? England is with him. I do not know who also is in the party. Neither do I care. I do not like it a little bit. Jealous? The idea. Just plain furious. I am no more afraid of Jack falling in love with another woman than I am of Saturn making Venus a birthday present of one of his rings. The trouble is she may fall in love with him, and it is altogether unnecessary for any other woman to get her feelings disturbed over Jack.

153

The Lady and Sada San

I fail to see the force of his argument that it is not safe nor wise for any woman in that country, and yet for him to show wild enthusiasm over the presence of the Britisher. No, Jack has lost his head over intellect. It may take a good sharp blow for him to realize that intellect, pure and simple, is an icy substitute for love. Like most men he is so deadly sure of one, he is taking a holiday with the other.

Of course you are laughing at me. So would Jack. And both would say it is unworthy. That's just it. It is the measly little unworthies that nag one to desperation. Besides, Mate, I shrink from any more trouble, any more heart-aches as I would from flames. The terror of the by-gone years creeps over me and covers the present like a pall.

There is only one thing left to do.

154

The Lady and Sada San

Work. Work and dig, till there is not
an ounce of strength left for worry. I
stay in the kindergarten every available minute. The unstinted friendship
of the kiddies over there, is the heart's-
ease for so many of life's hurts.

There are always the long walks,
when healing and uplift of spirit can
be found in the beauty of the country.
I tramp away all alone. The little
Swede begs often to go. At first I
rather enjoyed him. But he is growing
far too affectionate. I am not equal to
caring for *two* young things; a broken-
hearted girl *and* a homesick fat boy are
too much for me. He is improving so
rapidly I think it better for him to talk
love stories and poetry to some one
more appreciative. I am not in a very
poetical mood. He might just as well
talk to the pretty young teacher as
to talk about her all the time.

The Lady and Sada San

I have scores of friends up and down the many country roads I travel. The boatmen on the silvery river, who always wave their head rags in salute, the women hoeing in the fields with babies on their backs, stop long enough to say good day and good luck. The laughing red-cheeked coolie girls pause in their work of driving piles for the new bridge to have a little talk about the wonders of a foreigner's head. With bated breath they watch while I give them proof that my long hatpins do not go straight through my skull.

The sunny greetings of multitudes of children lift the shadows from the darkest day, and always there is the glorious scenery; the shadowed mystery of the mountains, a turquoise sky, the blossoms and bamboo. The brooding spirit of serenity soon envelops me, and in its irresistible charm is found a tender peace.

On my way home, in the river close to shore, is a crazy little tea-house. It is furnished with three mats and a paper lantern. The pretty hostess, fresh and sweet from her out-of-door life, brings me rice, tea and fresh eel. She serves it with such gracious hospitality it makes my heart warm. While I eat, she tells me stories of the river life. I am learning about the social life of families of fish and their numerous relatives that sport in the "Thing of Substance River"; the habits of the red-headed wild ducks which nest near; of the god and goddesses who rule the river life, the pranks they play, the revenge they take. And, too, I am learning a lesson in patience through the lives of the

humble fishermen. In season seven
cents a day is the total of their earn-
ings. At other times, two cents is the
limit. On this they manage to live and
laugh and raise a family. It is all so
simple and childlike, so free from pre-
tension, hurry and rush. Sometimes I
wonder if it is not we, with our myriad
interests, who have strayed from the
real things of life.

On my road homeward, too, there is
a crudely carved Buddha. He is so altogether hideous, they have put him in
a cage of wooden slats. On certain
days it is quite possible to try your
fortune, by buying a paper prayer
from the priest at the temple, chewing
it up and throwing it through the cage
at the image. If it sticks you will be
lucky.

My aim was not straight or luck was
against me to-day. My prayers are all

on the floor at the feet of the grinning Buddha.

Jack is in Siberia and Uncle has Sada. I have not heard from her since she left. I am growing truly anxious.

January, 1912.

Dearest Mate:

At last I have a letter from Jack. Strange to say I am about as full of enthusiasm over the news he gives me as a thorn-tree is of pond-lilies.

He says he has something like a ton of notes and things on the various stunts of the bubonic germ in Manchuria when it is feeling fit and spry. But he is seized with a conviction that he must go somewhere in northwest China where he thinks there is happy hunting-ground of evidence which will verify his report to the Government.

159

The Lady and Sada San

Suppose the next thing I hear he will be chasing around the outer rim of the old world hunting for somebody to verify the Government.

There is absolutely no use of my trying to say the name of the place he has started for. Even when written it looks too wicked to pronounce. It is near the Pass that leads into the Gobi Desert.

Jack wrote me to go to Shanghai and he would join me later. I am writing him that I can't start till the fate of Sada San is settled for better or for worse.

Nankow, China. February, 1912.

Mate:

News of Jack's desperate illness came to me ten days ago and has laid waste my heart as the desert wind blasts life. I have been flying to him as fast as boat and train and cart will take me.

The second wire reached me in Peking last night. Jack has typhus fever and the disease is nearing the crisis. I have read the message over and over, trying to read between the lines some faint glimmer of hope; but I can get no comfort from the noncommittal words except the fact that Jack is still alive. I am on my way to the terminus of the railroad, from where the message was sent. I came this far by train, only to find all regular traffic stopped by order of the Government. The line may be needed for the escape of the Imperial Family from Peking if the Palace is threatened by the revolutionists.

Orders had been given that no foreigner should leave the Legation enclosure. I bribed the room boy to slip me through the side streets and dark alleys to an outside station. I must go the rest of the distance by cart when the road is possible, by camel or donkey when not. Nothing seems possible now. Everything within sight looks as if it had been dead for centuries, and the people walking around have just forgotten to be buried.

I am wild with impatience to be gone but neither bribes nor threats will hurry the coolies who take their time harnessing the donkeys and the camels.

A ring of ossified men, women and children have formed about me, staring with unblinking eyes, till I feel as if I was full of peep holes. It is not life, for neither youth nor love nor sorrow has ever passed this way. The tiniest emotion would shrivel if it dared begin to live. Maybe they are better so. But then, they have never known Jack.

How true it is that one big heart-ache

withers up all the little ones and the joy of years as well. With this terror upon me, even Sada's desperate trouble has faded and grown pale as the memory of a dream. Jack is ill and I must get to him, though my body is racked with the rough travel, and the ancient road holds the end of love and life for me.

Around the sad old world I am stretching out my arms to you, Mate, for the courage to face whatever comes, and your love which has never failed me.

KALGAN.

Such wild unbelievable things have happened!

After twenty miles of intolerable shaking on the back of a camel, my battered body fell off at the last stopping-place, which happened to be here. There is no hotel. But three blessed

The Lady and Sada San

European boys living at this place—
agents for a big tobacco firm—took me
into their little home. From that time
—ten days ago—till now, they have
served and cared for me as only sons
who have not forgotten their mothers
could do.

On that awful night I came, while
forcing food on me, they said that Jack
had stopped with them on his way out
to the desert, where he was to complete
his work for the Government. He was
to go part of the distance with the English woman, who, with her camels and
her guides, was traveling to the Siberian railroad. The next day they
heard the whole caravan had returned.
Four days out Jack had been taken ill.
The only available shelter was an old
monastery about a mile from the village. To this he had been moved. My
hosts opened a window and pointed to

a far-away, high-up light. It was like the flicker of a match in a vast cave of darkness. They told me wonderful things of the rooms in the monastery, which were cut in the solid rock of the mountain-side, and the strange dwarf priest who kept it.

They lied beautifully and cheerfully as to Jack's condition, and all the time in their hearts they knew that he had the barest chance to live through the night.

The woman doctor had nursed him straight through, permitting no one else near. The dwarf priest brought her supplies.

Her last message for the day had been, "The crisis will soon be passed."

Even now something grips my throat when I remember how those dear boys worked to divert me, until my strength revived. They rigged up a battered steamer-chair with furs and bath robes, put me in it, promising that as soon as I was rested they would see what could be done to get me up to the monastery. But I was not to worry. All of them set about seeing I had no time to think. Each took his turn in telling me marvelous tales of the life in that wild country. One boy brought in the new litter of puppies, begging me to carefully choose a name for each. The two ponies were trotted out and put through their pranks before the door in the half light of a dim lantern.

They showed me the treasures of their bachelor life, the family photographs and the various little nothings which link isolated lives to home and love. They even assured me they had had *the* table-cloth and napkins washed for my coming. Household interests exhausted, they began to talk of boy-

The Lady and Sada San

hood days. Their quiet voices soothed me. From exhaustion I slept. When I woke, my watch said one o'clock. The house was heavy with sleeping stillness.

Through my window, far away the dim light wavered. It seemed to be signaling me. My decision was quick. I would go, and alone. If I called, my hosts would try to dissuade me, and I would not listen. For life or for death, I was going to Jack. The very thought lent me strength and gave my feet cunning stealthiness. A high wall was around the house but, thank Heaven, they had forgotten to lock the gate.

Soon I was in the deserted, deep-rutted street shut in on either side by mud hovels, low and crouching close together in their pitiful poverty. There was nothing to guide me, save that distant speck of flame. Further on, I heard the rush of water and made out the dim line of an ancient bridge. Half way across I stumbled. From the heap of rags my foot had struck, came moans, and, by the sound of it, awful curses. It was a handless leper. I saw the stumps as they flew at me. Sick with horror, I fled and found an open place.

The light still beckoned. The way was heavy with high, drifted sand. The courage of despair goaded me to the utmost effort. Forced to pause for breath, I found and leaned against a post. It was a telegraph pole. In all the blackness and immeasurable loneliness, it was the solitary sign of an inhabited world. And the only sound was the wind, as it sang through the taut wires in the unspeakable sadness of minor chords. A camel cara-

van came by, soft-footed, silent and inscrutable. I waited till it passed out
to the mysteries of the desert beyond
the range of hills.

I began again to climb the path. It
was lighter when I crept through a
broken wall and found myself in a stone
courtyard, with gilded shrines and
grinning Buddhas. One image more
hideous than the rest, with eyes like
glow-worms, untangled its legs and
came towards me. I shook with fright.
But it was only the dwarf priest—a
monstrosity of flesh and blood, who
kept the temple. I pointed to the light
which seemed to be hanging to the side
of the rocks above. He slowly shook
his head, then rested it on his hands
and closed his eyes. I pushed him
aside and painfully crawled up the
shallow stone stairs, and found a door
at the top. I opened it. Lying on a

stone bed was Jack, white and still. A woman leaned over him with her hand on his wrist. Her face was heavily lined with a long life of sorrow. On her head was a crown of snow-white hair. She raised her hand for silence. I fell at her feet a shaking lump of misery.

I could not live through it again, Mate—those remaining hours of agony, when every second seemed the last for Jack. But morning dawned, and with the miracle of a new-born day came the magic gift of life. When Jack opened his eyes and feebly stretched out his hand to me, my singing heart gave thanks to God.

And so the crisis was safely passed. And the hateful science I believed was taking Jack from me, in the skilful hands of a good woman, gave him back to me.

The one comfort left me in the humiliation of my petty, unreasoning jealousy—yes, I *had* been jealous—was to tell her.

And she, whose name was Edith Bowden, opened to me the door of her secret garden, wherein lay the sweet and holy memories of her lover, dead in the long ago.

For forty long and lonesome years she had unfalteringly held before her the vision of her young sweetheart and his work, and through them she had toiled to make reàl his ideals.

I take it all back, Mate. A career that makes such women as this is a beautiful and awesome thing.

In spite of all my pleadings to come with us, Miss Bowden started once again on her lonely way across the wind-swept plains, back to Europe and her work, leaving me with a never-to-be-forgotten humility of spirit and an homage in my heart that never before have I paid a woman.

I am too polite to say it, but I have had a taste of the place you spell with four letters. Also of Heaven. Just now, with Jack's thin hand safely in mine, I am hovering around the doors of Paradise in the house of the boys in Kalgan. If you could see the dusty little Chinese-Mongolian village, hanging on the upper lip of the mouth of the Gobi Desert, you would think it a strange place to find bliss. But joy can beautify sand and Sodom.

Yesterday my hosts made me take a ride out into the Desert. Oh, Mate, in spots these glittering golden sands are sublime. My heart was so light and the air so rare, it was like flying through sunlit space on a legless horse.

Life, or what answers to it, has been going on in the same way since thousands of years before Pharaoh went on that wild lark to the Red Sea. Every minute I expected to see Abraham and Sarah trailing along with their flocks and their families, hunting a place to stake out a claim, and Noah somewhere on a near-by sand-hill, taking in tickets for the Ark Museum, while the "two by two's" fed below. I never heard of these friends being in this part of the country, but you can never tell what a wandering spirit will do.

Jack is getting fat laughing at me. But Jack never was a lady and does not know what havoc imagination and the spell of the East can play with a loving but lonesome wife. And take it from me, beloved, he never will. Nothing gained in exposing all your follies.

He sends love to you. So do I—from the joyful heart of a woman whose most terrible troubles never happened.

PEKING, February, 1912.

Mate:

I do not know whether I can write you sanely or not. But write you I must. It is my one outlet in these days of anxious waiting. I have just cabled Billy Milton, in Nebraska, to come by the first steamer. I have not an idea what he will do when he gets to Japan, or how I will help him; but he is my one hope.

Yesterday, on our arrival here, I found a desperate letter from Sada San, written hurriedly and sent secretly. She finds that the man Hara, whom her uncle has promised she shall

174

marry, has a wife and three children!

The man, on the flimsiest pretext, has sent the woman home to clear his establishment for the new wife. And, Mate, can you believe it, he has kept the children—the youngest a nursing baby, just three months old!

One of the geisha girls in the teahouse slipped in one night and told Sada. She went at once to Uncle and asked him if it was true. He said that it was, and that Sada should consider herself very lucky to be wanted by such a man. Upon Sada telling him she would die before she would marry the man, he laughed at her. Since then she has not been permitted to leave her room.

The lucky day for marriage has been found and set. Thank goodness, it is seventeen days from now, and if Billy races across by Vancouver he can make it. In the meantime Nebraska seems a million miles away. I know the heart-beats of the fellow who is riding to the place of execution, with a reprieve. But seventeen days is a deadly slow nag.

I had already told Jack of my anxiety for Sada San and of the fate that was hanging over her, but now that the blow has suddenly fallen I dare not tell him. In a situation like this I know what Jack would want to do; and in his present weakened condition it might be fatal.

It is useless for me to appeal to anybody out here. Those in Japan who would help are powerless. Those who could help would smile serenely and tell me it was the law. And law and custom supersede any lesser question of right or wrong. By it the smallest act of every inhabitant is regulated, from the quantity of air he breathes to the proper official place for him to die. But, imagine the *majesty* of any law which makes it a ghastly immorality to mildly sass your mother-in-law, and a right, lawful and moral act for a man, with any trumped-up excuse, to throw his legal wife out of the house, that room may be made for another woman who has appealed to his fancy.

Japan may not need missionaries, but, by all the Mikados that ever were or will be, her divorce laws need a few revisions more than the nation needs battleships. You might run a country without gunboats, but never without women.

This case of Hara is neither extreme nor unusual. I have been face to face in this flowery kingdom with tragedies of this kind when a woman was the blameless victim of a man's caprice, and he was upheld by a law that would shame any country the sun shines on. By a single stroke of a pen through her name, on the records at the court-house, the woman is divorced—sometimes before she knows it. Then she goes away to hide her disgrace and her broken heart—not broken because of her love for the man who has cast her off, but because, from the time she is invited to go home on a visit and her clothes are sent after her, on through life, she is marked. If she has children, the chances are that the husband retains possession of them, and she is seldom, if ever, permitted to see them.

I know your words of caution would be, Mate, not to be rash in my condemnations, to remember the defects of my own land. I am neither forgetful nor rash. I do not expect to reform the country, neither am I arguing. I am simply telling you facts.

I know, too, that some Fountain Head of knowledge will rise from the back seat and beg to state that the new civil code contains many revisions and regulates divorce. The only trouble with the new civil code is that it keeps on containing the revisions and only in theory do they get beyond the books in which they are written.

Next to my own, in my affections, stands this sunlit, flower-covered land which has given the world men and women unselfishly brave and noble. But there are a few deformities in the country's law system that need the knife of a skilled surgeon, amputating right up to the last joint; among these the divorce laws made in ancient times by the gone-to-dust but still sacred and revered ancestors. Who would give a hang for any old ancestor so cut on the bias?

I cannot write any more. I am too agitated to be entertaining.

I wrote Sada a revised version of Blue Beard that would turn that venerable gentleman gray, could he read it. Uncle will be sure to. I dare him to solve the puzzle of my fancy writing. But I made Sada San know the Prince Red Head was coming to her rescue, if the engine did not break down.

Now there is nothing to do but wait and pray there are no weak spots in Billy's backbone.

Cable just received. William is on the wing!

PEKING, CHINA, February, 1912.

Well, here we still are, my convalescent Jack and I, bottled up in the middle of a revolution, and poor, helpless

180

The Lady and Sada San

little Sada San calling to me across the waters. Verily, these are strenuous days for this perplexed woman.

It is a tremendous sight to look out upon the incomprehensible saffron-hued masses that crowd the streets. I no longer wonder at the color of the Yellow Sea.

But, Oh, Mate, if I could only make you see the gilded walled city, in which history of the ages is being laid in dust and ashes, while the power that made it is hastening down the back alley to a mountain nunnery for safety! Peking is like a beautiful golden witch clothed in priceless garments of dusty yellow, girded with ropes of pearls. Her eyes are of jade, and so fine is the powdered sand she sifts from her tapering fingers it turns the air to an amber haze; so potent its magic spell, it fascinates and enthralls, while it repels.

The Lady and Sada San

For all the centuries the witch has held the silken threads, which bound her millions of subjects, she has been deaf —deaf to the cries of starvation, injustice and cruelty; heedless to devastation of life by her servants; smiling at piles of headless men; gloating over torture when it filled her treasure-house.

Ever cruel and heartless, now she is all a-tremble and sick with fear of the increasing power of the mighty young giant—Revolution. She sees from afar her numbered days. She is crying for the mercy she never showed, begging for time she never granted. She is a tottering despot, a dying tyrant, but still a beautiful golden witch.

We have not been here long but my soul has been sickened by the sights of the pitiless consequences of even the rumors of war all over the country and particularly in Peking. If only the responsible ones could suffer. But it is the poor, the innocent and the old who pay the price for the greed of the others. In this, how akin the East is to the West! The night we came there was a run on the banks caused by the report that Peking was to be looted and burned. Crowds of men, women and even children, hollow-eyed and haggard, jammed the streets before the doors of the banks, pleading for their little all. Some of them had as much as two dollars stored away! But it was the twenty dimes that deferred slow starvation. Banks kept open through the night. Officials and clerks worked to exhaustion, satisfying demands, hoping to placate the mob and avert the unthinkable results of a riot. Countless soldiers swarmed the streets with fixed bayonets. But the bloodless witch has no claim to one sin-

gle heart-beat of loyalty from the un-
paid wretches who wear the Imperial
uniform; and when by simply tying a
white handkerchief on their arms they
go over in groups of hundreds to the
Revolutionists, they are only repaying
treachery in its own foul coin.

Though I hate to leave Jack even for
an hour, I have to get out each day for
some fresh air. To-day it seemed to
me, as I walked among the crowds, fantastic in the flickering flames of bon-
fires and incandescent light, that life
had done its cruel worst to these people—had written her bitterest tokens
of suffering and woe in the deeply fur-
rowed faces and sullenly hopeless eyes.

Earlier in the year thousands of
farmers and small tradesmen had come
in from the country to escape floods,
famine and robber-bands. Hundreds
had sold their children for a dollar or

so and for days lived on barks and leaves, as they staggered toward Peking for relief.

Now thousands more are rushing from the city to the hills or to the desert, fleeing from riot and war, the strong carrying the sick, the young the old—each with a little bundle of household goods, all camping near the towering gates in the great city wall, ready to dash through when the keeper flings them open in the early morning.

And through it all the merciless execution of any suspect or undesirable goes merrily on. Close by my carriage a cart passed. In it were four wretched creatures with hands and feet bound and pigtails tied together. They were on their way to a plot of crimson ground where hundreds part with their heads. By the side of the cart ran a ten-year-old boy, his uplifted

face distorted with agony of grief.
One of the prisoners was his father.

I watched the terrified masses till a
man and woman of the respectable
farmer class came by, with not enough
rags on to hide their half-starved bodies. Between them they carried on
their shoulders a bamboo pole, from
which was swung a square of matting.
On this, in rags, but clean, lay a mere
skeleton of a baby with beseeching eyes
turned to its mother; and from its lips
came piteous little whines like a hun-
ger-tortured kitten. Tears streamed
down the woman's cheeks as she
crooned and babbled to the child in a
language only a tender mother knows,
but in her eyes was the look of a soul
crucified with helpless suffering.

I slipped all the money I had into the
straw cradle and fled to our room.
Jack was asleep. I got into my bed

and covered up my head to shut out the horrors of the multitude that are hurting my own heart like an eternal toothache.

But, honey, bury me deep when there is n't a smile lurking around the darkest corner. Neither war nor famine can wholly eliminate the comical. Yesterday afternoon some audacious youngsters asked me to chaperon a tea-party up the river. We went in a gaily decorated house-boat, made tea on a Chinese stove of impossible shape, and ate cakes and sandwiches innumerable. Aglow with youth and its joys, reckless of danger, courting adventure, the promoters of the enterprise failed to remember that we were outside the city walls, that the gates were closed at sunset and nothing but a written order from an official could open them. We had no such order. When it was quite dark, we faced entrances doubly locked and barred. The guardian inside might have been dead for all he heeded our importunities and bribes. At night outside the huge pile of brick and stone, inclosing and guarding the city from lawless bandits, life is not worth a whistle. A dismayed little giggle went round the crowd of late tea revelers as we looked up the twenty-five feet of smooth wall topped by heavy battlements. Just when we had about decided that our only chance was to stand on each other's shoulders and try to hack out footholds with a bread knife, some one suggested that we try the effect of college yells on the gentlemen within. Imagine the absurdity of a dozen terrified Americans standing there in the heart of China yelling in unison for Old Eli, and Nassau, and the Harvard Blue!

The Lady and Sada San

The effect was magical. Curiosity is one of the strongest of Oriental traits, and before long the gates creaked on their hinges and a crowd of slant-eyed, pig-tailed heads peered wonderingly out. The rest was easy, and I heard a great sigh of relief as I marshaled my little group into safety.

Jack's many friends here in Peking are determined that I shall have as good a time as possible. Worried by disorganized business, harassed with care, they always find opportunity not only to plan for my pleasure but see that I have it, properly attended—for of course Jack is not yet able to leave his room.

Beyond the power of any man is the prophecy of what may happen to official-ridden Peking. The air is surcharged with mutterings. The brutally oppressed people may turn at last, rise, and, in their fury, rend to bits all flesh their skeleton fingers grasp.

The Legations grouped around the hotel are triply guarded. The shift, shift, shift of soldiers' feet as they march the streets rubs my nerves like sandpaper.

Rest and sleep are impossible. We seem constantly on the edge of a precipice, over which, were we to go, the fate awaiting us would reduce the tortures of Hades to pin-pricks. The Revolutionists have the railroads, the bandits the rivers. Yet, if I don't reach Japan in twelve days now, I will be too late. Poor Sada San!

Please say to your small son David that his request to send him an Emperor's crown to wear when he plays king, is not difficult to grant. At the present writing crowns in the Orient are not fashionable. As I look out of my window, the salmon-pink walls of the Forbidden City rise in the dusty distance. Under the flaming yellow roof of the Palace is a frail and frightened little six-year-old boy—the ruler of millions —who, if he knew and could, would gladly exchange his priceless crown for freedom and a bag of marbles.

Good night.

PEKING, Next day.

It is Sunday afternoon and pouring rain. Outside it is so drearily mournful, I keep my back turned. At least, the dripping wet will secure me a quiet hour or so.

My Chinese room-boy reasons that only a sure-enough somebody would have so many callers and attend so many functions—not knowing that it is only because Jack's wife will never lack where he has friends. Hence the boy haunts my door ready to serve and reap his reward. But I am sure it was only kindness that prompted him on this dreary day to set the fire in the grate to blazing and arrange the tea-table, the steaming kettle close by, and turn on all the lights. How cozy it is! How homelike!

Jack grows stronger each day, and crosser, which is a good sign. At last I have told him of Sada San's plight; and he is for starting for Kioto to-morrow to "wipe the floor with Uncle Mura," as he elegantly expresses it. But of course he's still too weak to even think of such a journey.

He makes me join in the gaieties that still go on despite the turmoil and unrest. I must tell you of one dinner which, of the many brilliant functions, was certainly unique.

It was a sumptuous affair given by

one of the Legation officials. I wore
my glory dress—the color Jack loves
best. I went in a carriage guarded on
the outside by soldiers. Beside me sat
a strapping European with his pockets
bulging suspiciously. I was not in the
least afraid of the threatening mob
which stopped us twice.

I could almost have welcomed an attack, just to get behind my big escort
and see him clear the way.

Merciful powers! Hate is a sweet
and friendly word for what the masses
feel for the foreigners, whom most believe to be in league with the Government.

Happily, nothing more serious happened than breaking all the carriage
windows; and, in the surprise that
awaited me in the drawing-room of the
gorgeously appointed mansion, I quite
forgot that.

The Lady and Sada San

Who should be almost the first to greet me but Dolly and Mr. Dolly, otherwise the Seeker, married and on their honeymoon! She was radiant. And oh, Mate, if you could only see the change in him! As revolutions seem to be in order, Dolly has worked a prize one on him, I think. He was positively gentle and showed signs of the making of a near gentleman. I was glad to see them, and more than glad to see Dolly's unfeigned happiness. The mournful little prince has gone on his way to lonely, isolated Sikkam to take up his task of endless reincarnation.

Very soon I found another surprise —my friend Mr. Carson of the Rockies. It seemed a little incongruous that the simple, unlettered Irishman should have found his way into the brilliant, many-countried company, where were men who made history and held the fate

of nations in their hands and built or
crumbled empires, and women to match,
regally gowned, keen of wit and wisdom.

But, bless you, he was neither troubled nor out of place. He was the es-
sence of democracy and mixed with the
guests with the same innocent simplicity that he would have shown at his
village church social.

He greeted me cordially, asked after
Jack and spoke enthusiastically of his
work.

I smiled when I saw that in the curious shuffling of cards he had been
chosen as the dinner escort of a tall
and stately Russian beauty. I watched
them walk across the waxen floor and
heard him say to her, "Sure if I had
time I would telegraph for me roller
skates to guide ye safely over the slick-
ness of the boards." Her answering

laugh, sweet and friendly, was reassuring.

For a while it was a deadly solemn feast. The difficulty was to find topics of common interest without stumbling upon forbidden subjects. You see, Mate, times are critical; and the only way to keep out of trouble is not to get in by being too wordy. By my side sat a stern-visaged leader of the Revolution. Across the way, a Manchu Prince.

Mr. Carson and the beauty were just opposite. I became absorbed in watching her exquisite tact in guiding the awkward hands of her partner through the silver puzzle on each side of his plate to the right eating utensils at the proper time. I saw her pleased interest in all his talk, whether it was crops, cider or pigtails. And for her gentle

The Lady and Sada San

courtesy and kindness to my old friend
I blessed her and wiped out a big score
I had against her country. How glad
Russia will be!

But the Irishman was not happy.
Course after course had been served.
With every rich course came a rare
wine. Colorado shook a shaggy gray
head at every bottle, though he was
choking with thirst. He was a teeto-
taler. Whenever boy No. 1, who served
the wine, approached, he whispered,
"Water." It got to be "Water,
please, *water!*" Then threateningly,
"Water, blame ye! Fetch me water."
It was vain pleading. At best a Chinaman is no friend to water; and when
the word is flung at him with an Emerald accent it fails to arrive. But ten
courses without moisture bred desperation; and all at once, down the length

of that banquet board, went a hoarsely whispered plea, in the richest imaginable brogue,

"Hostess, *where's* the pump?"

It was like a sky-rocket scattering showers of sparks on a lowering cloud. In a twinkling the heaviness of the feast was dispersed by shouts of laughter. Everybody found something delightful to tell that was not dangerous.

We wound up by going to a Chinese theater. When we left, after two hours of death and devastation, the demands of the drama for gore were still so great, assistants had to be called from out the audience to change the scenery and dead men brought to life to go on with the play.

When I got back Jack was, of course, asleep; but he had been busy in my absence. I found a note on my pincushion saying he had sent a wire to

meet Billy's steamer on its arrival at
Yokohama and that I 'm to start alone
for Japan in a day or two—as soon as
it seems safe to travel.

Next day.

Honey, there is a thrill a minute. I
may not live to see the finish, for the
soldiers have mutinied and joined the
mob, maddened with lust for blood and
loot. I must tell you about it while I
can; for it is not every day one has the
chance of seeing a fresh and daring
young Republic sally up to an all-pow-
erful dynasty, centuries old with
tyranny and treasure, and say, "Now,
you vamoose the Golden Throne. It
matters not where you go, but hustle;
and I don't want any back talk while
you are doing it."

If I was n't so excited I might be
nervous. But, Mate, when you see a

cruelly oppressed people winning their freedom with almost nothing to back them but plain grit, you want to sing, dance, pray and shout all at the same time, and there is no mistake about young China having a mortgage on all the surplus nerve of the country. Of course, the mob, awful as it is, is simply an unavoidable attachment of war.

All day there has been terrible fighting, and I am told the streets are blocked with headless bodies and plunder that could not be carried off.

The way the mob and the soldier-bandits got into the city is a story that makes any tale of the Arabian Nights fade away into dull myth.

Some years ago a Manchu official, high in command, espied a beautiful flower-girl on the street and forthwith attached her as his private property. So great was her fascination, the tables

were turned and he became the slave—
till he grew tired. He not only scorned
her, but he deserted her. Though a
Manchu maid, the Revolution played
into her tapering fingers the opportunity for the sweetest revenge that
ever tempted an almond-eyed beauty.
It had been the proud boast of her offi-
cer master that he could resist any at-
tacking party and hold the City Royal
for the Manchus. Alas! he reckoned
without a woman. She knew a man
outside the city walls—a leader of an
organization—half soldiery, half bandits—who thirsted for the chance to pay
off countless scores against officers and
private citizens inside. After a vain
effort to win back her lover, the flower-
girl communicated with the captain of
the rebel band, who had only been de-
terred from entering the city by a high
wall twenty feet thick. She told him to

be ready to come in on a certain night—
the gates would be open. The night
came. She slipped from doorway to
doorway through the guarded streets
till she reached the appointed place.
Even the sentries unconsciously lent a
hand to her plan, in leaving their posts
and seeking a tea-house fire by which to
warm their half-frozen bodies. The
one-time jewel of the harem, who had
seldom lifted her own teacup, tugged at
the mighty gates with her small hands
till the bars were raised and in rushed
the mob. She raced to her home,
decked herself in all the splendid jewels
he had given her, stuck red roses in her
black hair, and stood on a high roof and
jeered her lover as he fled for his life
through the narrow streets.

The city is bright with the fires
started by the rabble. The yellow

roofs, the pink walls and the towering marble pagodas catch the reflection of the flames, making a scene of barbaric splendor that would reduce the burning of Rome to a feeble little bonfire.

The pitiful, the awful and the very funny are so intermixed, my face is fatally twisted trying to laugh and cry at the same time. Right across from my window, on the street curbing, a Chinaman is getting a hair-cut. In the midst of all the turmoil, hissing bullets and roaring mobs, he sits with folded hands and closed eyes as calm as a Joss, while a strolling barber manipulates a pair of foreign shears. For him blessed freedom lies not in the change of Monarchy to Republic, but in the shearing close to the scalp the hated badge of bondage— his pigtail.

And, Mate, the first thing the loot-

ers do when they enter a house is to
snatch down the telephones and take
them out to burn; for, as one rakish
bandit explained, they were the talking-
machines of the foreign devils and, if
left, might reveal the names of the loot-
ers!

High-born ladies with two-inch feet
stumble by, their calcimined faces
streaked with tears and fright. Gray-
haired old men shiver with terror and
try to hide in any small corner. Lost
children and deserted ones, frantic with
fear, cling to any passer-by, only to be
shoved into the street and often tram-
pled underfoot. And through it all, the
mob runs and pitilessly mows down
with sword and knife as it goes, and
plunders and sacks till there is nothing
left.

As I stood watching only a part of
this horror, I heard a long-haired

brother near me say, as he kept well under cover, "Inscrutable Providence!" But (my word!) I don't think it fair to lay it all on Providence.

So far the foreign Legations have been well guarded. But there is no telling how long the overworked soldiers can hold out. When they cannot, the Lord help the least one of us.

Jack's friends are working day and night, guarding their property.

I guess the Seeker found more of the plain unvarnished Truth in the East than he bargained for. He and Dolly have disappeared from Peking.

Nobody undresses these nights and few go to bed. Our bodyguard is the room-boy. I asked him which side he was on, and without a change of feature he answered, "Manchu Chinaman. Allee samee bimeby, Missy, I make you tea." I have a suspicion that he sleeps

The Lady and Sada San

across our door, for his own or our protection, I am not sure which; but sometimes, when the terrible howls of fighters reach me, as I doze in a chair, I turn on the light and sit by my fire to shake off a few shivers, trying to make believe I'm home in Kentucky, while Jack sleeps the sleep of the convalescent. Then a soft tap comes at my door and a very gentle voice says, "Missy, I make you tea." Shades of Pekoe! I'll drown if this keeps up much longer. He comes in, brews the leaves, then drops on his haunches and looks into the fire. Not by the quiver of an eyelash does he give any sign, no matter how close the shots and shouts. Inscrutable and immovable, he seems a thing utterly apart from the tremendous upheaval of his country. And yet, for all anybody knows, he may be chief plotter of the whole movement. His unmoved serenity is about the most soothing thing in all this Hades. I am not really and truly afraid. Jack is with me, and just over there, above the crimson glare of the burning city, gently but surely float the Stars and Stripes.

Good night, beloved Mate. I will not believe we are dead till it happens. Besides, I simply could not die till Jack and I have saved Sada San.

By the way, I start for Japan to-morrow. The prayers of the congregation are requested!

KIOTO HOTEL, KIOTO, March, 1912.
Beloved Mate:

Rejoice with me! Sing psalms and give thanks. Something has happened. I do not know just what it is, but little

207

thrills of happiness are playing hop-scotch up and down my back, and my head is lighter than usual.

Be calm and I will tell you about it.

In the first place, I got here this morning, more dead than alive, after days of travel that are now a mere blur of yelling crowds, rattling trains and heaving seas. A wire from Yokohama was waiting. Billy had beat me here by a few hours. At noon, to-day, a big broad-shouldered youth met me, whom I made no mistake in greeting as Mr. Milton. Billy's eyes are beautifully brown. William's chin looks as if it was modeled for the purpose of dealing with tea-house Uncles.

Not far from the station is a black-and-tan temple—ancient and restful. To that we strolled and sat on the edge of the Fountain of Purification, which faces the quiet monastery garden, while we talked things over. That is, Billy did the questioning; I did the talking to the mystic chanting of the priests.

I quickly related all that I knew of what had happened to Sada, and what was about to happen. There was no reason for me to adorn the story with any fringes for it to be effective. Billy's face was grim. He said little; put a few more questions, then left me saying he would join me at dinner in the hotel.

I passed an impatient, tedious afternoon. Went shopping, bought things I can never use, wondering all the time what was going to be the outcome. Got a reassuring cable from Jack in answer to mine, saying all was well with him.

Mr. Milton returned promptly this evening. He ordered dinner, then forgot to eat. He did not refer to the afternoon; and long intimacy with science has taught me when not to ask questions. There was only a fragment of a plan in my mind; I had no further communication from Sada, and knew nothing more than that the wedding was only a day off.

We decided to go to Uncle's house together. I was to get in the house and see Sada if possible, taking, as the excuse for calling, a print on which, in an absent-minded moment, I had squandered thirty yen.

Billy was to stay outside, and, if I could find the faintest reason for so doing, I was to call him in. This was his suggestion.

I found Uncle scintillating with good humor and hospitality. Evidently his plans were going smoothly; but not once did he refer to them. I asked for Sada. Uncle smiled sweetly and said she was not in. Ananias died for less!

210

The Lady and Sada San

He was quite capable of locking her up in some very quiet spot. I was externally indifferent and internally dismayed. I showed him my print. At once he was the eager, interested artist and he went into a long history of the picture.

Though I looked at him and knew he was talking, his words conveyed no meaning. I was faint with despair. It was my last chance. I could have wagered Uncle's best picture that Billy was tearing up gravel outside. I had been in the house an hour, and had accomplished nothing. Surely if I stayed long enough something had to happen.

Suddenly out of my hopelessness came a blessed thought. Uncle had once promised to show me a priceless original of Hokusai. I asked if I might see it then. He was so elated that without calling a servant to do it for him he disappeared into a deep cupboard to find his treasure.

For a moment, helpless and desperate, I was swayed with a mad impulse to lock him up in the cupboard; but there was no lock.

It was so deadly still it hurt. Then, coming from the outside, I heard a low whistle with an unmistakable American twist to it, followed by a soft scraping sound. My heart missed two beats. I did not know what was happening; nor was I sure that Sada was within the house; but something told me that my cue was to keep Uncle busy. I obeyed with a heavy accent. When he appeared with his print, I began to talk. I recklessly repeated pages of text-books, whether they fitted or not; I fired technical terms at him till he was dizzy with mental gymnastics.

212

The Lady and Sada San

He smoothed out his precious picture.
I fell upon it. I raved over the
straight-front mountains and the mar-
celed waves in that foolish old wood-
cut as I had never gushed over any
piece of paper before, and I hope I
never will again. Not once did he re-
linquish his hold of that faded deform-
ity in art, and neither did I.

Surely I surprised myself with the
new joys I constantly found in the pi-
geon-toed ladies and slant-eyed war-
riors. Uncle needed absorption, con-
centration and occupation. Mine was
the privilege to give him what he required.

No further sound from the garden
and the silence drilled holes into my
nerves. I was so fearful that the man
would see my trembling excitement, I
soon made my adieux.

Uncle seemed a little surprised and

graciously mentioned that tea was being prepared for me. I never wanted tea less and solitude more. I said I must take the night train for Hiroshima. It was a sudden decision; but to stay would be useless.

I said, "Sayonara," and smiled my sweetest. I had a feeling I would never see dear Uncle Mura on earth again and doubtless our environment will differ in the Beyond.

I went to the gate. It faced two streets. Both were empty. Not a sign of Billy nor the jinrickshas in which we had come. I trod on air as I tramped back to the hotel.

HIROSHIMA, Five Days Later, 1912.

Mate dear:

I am back in my old quarters—safe. Why should n't I be! A detective has been my constant companion since I left

The Lady and Sada San

Kioto, sitting by my berth all night on the train, and following me to the gates of the School!

I had planned to start back to Peking as soon as Sada and Billy were clear and away. But this detective business has made me very wary—not to say weary—and I've had to postpone my return to Jack to await the Emperor's pleasure and lest I bring more trouble on Sada's head, by following too closely on her heels; for I suspect the blessed elopers are themselves on the way to China.

When I took my walk into the country the afternoon after I got here, I saw the detective out of the back of my head, and a merry chase I led him—up the steepest paths I knew, down the rocky sides, across the ferry, and into the remote village, where I let him rest his body in the stinging cold while I made an unexpected call. For once he earned his salary and his supper.

That night I was in the sitting-room alone. A glass door leads out to an open porch. Conscious of a presence, I looked up to find two penetrating eyes fixed on me. It made me creepy and cold, yet I was amused. I sat long and late, but a quiet shadow near the door told me I was not alone. Even when in bed I could hear soft steps under my window.

I have just come from an interview that was deliciously illuminating.

Sada San has disappeared; and, so goes their acute reasoning, as I was the last person in Uncle's house, before her absence was discovered, the logical conclusion is that I have kidnapped her.

Two hours ago the scared housemaid came to announce that "two Mr. Soldiers with swords wanted to speak to me.''

I went at once, to find my guardian angel and the Chief of Police for this district in the waiting-room. We wasted precious minutes making inquiries about one another's health, accentuating every other word with a bow and a loud indrawn breath. We were tuning up for the business in hand.

The chief began by assuring me that I was a teacher of great learning. I had not heard it but bowed. It was poison to his spirit to question so honorable, august, and altogether wise a person, but I was suspected of a grave offense, and I must answer his questions.

Where was my home?

Easy.

How did I live?

Easier.

Who was my grandfather?

The Lady and Sada San

Fortunately I remembered.

Was I married?

Muchly.

Where was my master?

Did not have any. My husband was in China.

Was I in Japan by his permission?

I was.

Had I been sent home for disobedience? Please explain.

No explanation. I was just here.

Did I know the penalty for kidnaping?

No, color-prints interested me more.

Had any of my people ever been in the penitentiary?

No, only the Legislature.

At this both men looked puzzled. Then the Chief made a discovery.

"Ah-h," he sighed, "American word for crazysylum!"

Would Madame positively state that

she knew nothing of the girl's where-
abouts. Madame positively and truth-
fully so stated. I did not know. I only
knew what I thought; but, Mate, you
cannot arrest a man for thinking.
After a grilling of an hour or so they
left me, looking worried and perplexed.
They had never heard of Billy, and I
saw no use adding to their troubles.
Nobody seems to have noticed him at
dinner with me; and now that I think of
it, he had men strange to the hotel pull-
ing the jinrickshas.

It was dear of Billy not to implicate
me. I am ignorant of what really happened, but wherever they are I am sure
Sada is in the keeping of an honorable
man.

Last night, after I closed this letter,
I had a cable. It said:

"Married in heaven,

"BILLY AND SADA."

The Lady and Sada San

But the cables must have been crossed, for it was dated Shanghai; or else the operator was so excited over repeating such a message he forgot to put in the period.

March 15.

Just received a letter from Billy and Sada. It is a gladsome tale they tell. Young Lochinvar, though pale with envy, would bow to Billy's direct method. I can see you, blessed Mate that you are, smiling delightedly at the grand finale of the true love story I have been writing you these months. Billy says on the night it all happened he tramped up and down, waiting for me to call him, till he wore "gullies in the measly little old cow-path they call a street."

The passing moments only made him more furious. Finally he decided to walk right into the house, unannounced, and find Sada if he had to knock Uncle down and make kindling wood of the bamboo doll-house. But as he came into the side garden he saw in the second story a picture silhouetted on the white paper doors. It was Sada and her face was buried in her hands. That settled Billy. He would save Uncle all the worry of an argument by simply removing the cause. There in the dusk, he whistled the old college call, then swung himself up on a fat stone lantern, and in a few minutes he swung down a suitcase and Sada in American clothes. They caught a train to Kobe, which is only a short distance, and sailed out to the same steamer he had left in Yokohama and which arrived in Kobe that day.

Billy says, for a quick and safe wedding ceremony commend him to an enthusiastic, newly-arrived young missionary; and for rapid handling of red tape connected with a license, pin your faith to a fat and jolly American consul. So that was what the blessed rascal was doing all that afternoon he left me in Kioto to myself. Cannot you see success in life branded on William's freckled brow right now?

The story soon spread over the ship. Passengers and crew packed the music-room to witness the ceremony, and joyously drank the health of the lovers at the supper the Captain hastily ordered. Without hindrance, but half delirious with joy, they headed for Shanghai.

Billy found that he could transact a little business in China for the firm at home and with Western enterprise decided to make his honeymoon pay for itself.

And now that my task is finished I

shall follow them as fast as the next
steamer can carry me.

PEKING, APRIL, 1912.

Back once again, Mate, in the City of
Golden Dusts. Glorious spring sunshine, and the whole world wrapped in
a tender haze. Everything has little
rainbows around it and the very air is
studded with jewels.

Soldiers are still marching; flags are
flying; drums are thumping and it is
all to the tune of Victory for the Revolutionists. But best of all Jack is well!
To me Peking is like that first morning
of Eve's in the Garden of Eden.

What crowded, happy weeks these
last have been. Waiting for Jack;
amusing him when time hangs heavy—
even unto reading pages of scientific
books with words so big the spine of my
tongue is threatened with fracture.

The Lady and Sada San

And in between times? Well, I am thanking my stars for the chance to doubly make up for any little tenderness I may have passed by. Put it in your daily thought book, honey, forevermore I am going to remember that if at the time we'd use the strength in doing, that we consume afterwards being sorry we didn't do, life would run on an easy trolley.

Billy and Sada are with us, still with the first glow of the enchanted garden over them. Bless their happy hearts! I am going to give them my collection of color prints to start housekeeping with. How I'd *love* to see Uncle— through a telescope.

To-night we are having our last dinner here. To-morrow the four of us turn our faces toward the most beautiful spot this side of Heaven, home. The happy runaways to Nebraska, Jack

The Lady and Sada San

and I to the little roost we left behind
in Kentucky.

There goes the music for dinner.
It's something about "dreamy love."
Love isn't a dream, Mate—not the kind
I know; it's all of life and beyond.
I know what they are playing!

> Breathe but one breath
> Rose beauty above
> And all that was death
> Grows life, grows love,
> Grows love!

THE END